THE POWERBOOK

Jeanette Winterson is the author of *Oranges Are Not the Only Fruit*, *The Passion*, *Sexing the Cherry*, *Written on the Body*, *Art and Lies*, *Gut Symmetries*, *The World and Other Places* and a collection of essays, *Art Objects*.

ALSO BY JEANETTE WINTERSON

Fiction

Oranges Are Not the Only Fruit
The Passion
Sexing the Cherry
Written on the Body
Art & Lies
Gut Symmetries
The World and Other Places

Comic Book

Boating for Beginners

Non-Fiction

Art Objects

Screenplays

Oranges Are Not the Only Fruit (BBC TV)
Great Moments in Aviation (BBC TV)
The Passion (Miramax Films)

Jeanette Winterson

THE POWERBOOK

VINTAGE

Published by Vintage 2001

2 4 6 8 10 9 7 5 3 1

First published in Great Britain in 2000 by
Jonathan Cape

Vintage
Random House, 20 Vauxhall Bridge Road,
London SW1V 2SA

Random House Australia (Pty) Limited
20 Alfred Street, Milsons Point, Sydney
New South Wales 2061, Australia

Random House New Zealand Limited
18 Poland Road, Glenfield, Auckland 10,
New Zealand

Random House (Pty) Limited
Endulini, 5A Jubilee Road, Parktown 2193,
South Africa

The Random House Group Limited Reg. No. 954009
www.randomhouse.co.uk

A CIP catalogue record for this book
is available from the British Library

ISBN 0 09 928543 6

Printed and bound in Australia by
Griffin Press

To Peggy Reynolds with love

Thanks to Ruth Rendell, Suzanne Gluck, Caroline Michel,
Dan Franklin, Paul Shearer, Mizzi van der Pluijm, Erica
Wagner, Lisa Jardine, Philippa Brewster and Hilary Fairclough,
Marianna Kennedy, Dan Cruickshank, James Howett, and –
friends not here any more – Kathy Acker and Don Rendell.

MENU

language costumier

To avoid discovery I stay on the run. To discover things for myself I stay on the run.

It's night. I'm sitting at my screen. There's an e-mail for me. I unwrap it. It says – *Freedom, just for one night.*

Years ago you would have come to my shop at the end of the afternoon, telling your mother you had an errand for the poor.

At the tinkle of the bell you would have found yourself alone for a moment in the empty shop, looking at the suits of armour, the wimples, the field boots, and the wigs on spikes, like severed heads.

The sign on the shop says VERDE, nothing more, but everyone knows that something strange goes on inside. People arrive as themselves and leave as someone else. They say that Jack the Ripper used to come here.

You stand alone in the empty shop. I come out from the back. What is it you want?

Freedom for a night, you say. Just for one night the freedom to be somebody else.

Did anyone see you arrive?

No.

Then I can pull the blinds and light the lamp. The clock ticks, but only in time. From outside, looking in, there will be only a movement of shadows – the looming of a bear's head, a knife.

You say you want to be transformed.

This is where the story starts. Here, in these long lines of laptop DNA. Here we take your chromosomes, twenty-three pairs, and alter your height, eyes, teeth, sex. This is an invented world. You can be free just for one night.

Undress.

Take off your clothes. Take off your body. Hang them up behind the door. Tonight we can go deeper than disguise.

It's only a story, you say. So it is, and the rest of life with it – creation story, love story, horror, crime, the strange story of you and me.

The alphabet of my DNA shapes certain words, but the story is not told. I have to tell it myself.

What is it that I have to tell myself again and again?

That there is always a new beginning, a different end.

I can change the story. I am the story.

Begin.

OPEN HARD DRIVE

I want to start with a tulip.

In the sixteenth century the first tulip was imported to Holland from Turkey. I know – I carried it myself.

By 1634 the Dutch were so crazy for this fish-mouthed flower that one collector exchanged a thousand pounds of cheese, four oxen, eight pigs, twelve sheep, a bed and a suit of clothes for a single bulb.

What's so special about a tulip?

Put it this way . . . When is a tulip not a tulip?

When it's a Parrot or a Bizarre. When it's variegated or dwarf. When it comes called Beauty's Reward or Heart's Reviver. When it comes called Key of Pleasure or Lover's Dream . . .

Tulips, every one – and hundreds more – each distinctively different, all the same. The attribute of variation that humans and tulips share.

It was Key of Pleasure and Lover's Dream that I carried from

Sulyman the Magnificent to Leiden in 1591. To be exact, I strapped them under my trousers . . .

'Put it this way.'
    'No. I'll crush them when I rest.'
    'Put it this way . . .'
    'No. I'll crush them when I pray.'
    'Put one here and one here . . .'
    'No! It will look as though I have an evil swelling.'

Well, where would you store a priceless pair of bulbs?

That gave me the idea.

In the same place as a priceless pair of balls.

Yes! Yes! Yes!

When I was born, my mother dressed me as a boy because she could not afford to feed any more daughters. By the mystic laws of gender and economics, it ruins a peasant to place half a bowl of figs in front of his daughter, while his son may gorge on the whole tree, burn it for firewood and piss on the stump, and still be reckoned a blessing to his father.

    When I was born, my father wanted to drown me, but my mother persuaded him to let me live in disguise, to see if I could bring any wealth to the household.

I did.

So slender am I, and so slight, that I can slip under the door of a palace, or between the dirt and the floor of a hovel, and never be seen.

A golden thread, a moment's talk, a spill of coffee, a pepper seed, is all the distance I am between one side and the other.

I became a spy.

Sulyman himself appointed me and his instruction now is that I should get into a boat and bear a gift to his friends, the Dutch. A gift that every scurvy captain and leprous merchant will try to steal.

How to conceal it?

Put it this way . . .

My mother got some stout thread and belted it through the natural die-back of the bulb tops. Then she sewed the lot on to a narrow leather strap and fastened it round my hips.

'Should they hang dead centre like that?'

(My mother went to inspect my father.)

'Dress them on the left.'

'That's good, but there's something missing.'

'What?'

'The bit in the middle.'

I went up into the hills, for tulips grow as thick as thieves here. I found myself a well-formed fat stem supporting a good-sized red head with rounded tips. I nicked it at the base with my knife and the juice covered my fingers.

At home my mother embalmed the tulip, and in a few days it was ready to wear.

This was my centrepiece. About eight inches long, plump, with a nice weight to it. We secured it to my person and inspected the results. There are many legends of men being turned into beasts and women into trees, but none I think, till now, of a woman who becomes a man by means of a little horticultural grafting.

My mother knelt down and put her nose close.

'You smell like a garden,' she said.

The sun rose. The ship hoisted sail. I lifted my arms and waved and waved. Then, adjusting my tulip, I went below.

I seemed to dream of buffalo muddying the banks of clear streams that spilled down into the watercress beds. There were crystallised oranges on a table in the sun, and small cups of sweet coffee, and the little workshops and weaving sheds of our town.

There were women at the roadside selling hard-boiled eggs and homemade dolma, while their children wove simple mats and their men unloaded charcoal or packed tobacco, or went in and out of Nikolaus the pawnbroker's.

I dreamed I was ploughing a field and the stork was following behind me and inspecting the turned earth and waiting by the marshy edges for a frog.

At the bazaar, the copper pots were coming in stacked on the ox-carts. Eager hands carried them to shaded rugs, to burnish up the spatterings with a cloth. All the pots were sealed – it keeps the genie in, and no Turk would want a pot without a genie.

Humble or grand, what is made must keep with it the memory of what cannot be made. In the spun cloth, the thrown earthenware, the beaten pot and the silver box, is Allah – the spirit of God in the things of the world.

Atom and dream.

I awoke to a rattle. The only light in my cabin was a wick in a cruse of oil. I took it from the shelf over my hammock and looked down. I had filled a wooden bucket with water for washing and drinking, and left my metal cup on its chain inside the bucket. Knocking the cup from side to side as it drank was a long-haired rat.

In the morning, as the only paying passenger on the spice ship, I was invited to breakfast with the Captain. He offered me roast chicken and his wife's hard-baked bread covered in pumpkin seeds.

He was a man of the world and a worldly man, who profited from trade with the English, regularly cargoing the tin, coarse cloth and shot the Sultan needed for his armies, in return for the jewels and luxury stuffs the English loved.

If tin for gold and shot for rubies seems a strange exchange, blame the Pope. The Pope, not one but many Popes, the sum-total-continuous-Pope without beginning or end, had refused to allow his flock to trade with the Infidel, and since his flock was all Europe the Ottoman Empire had trouble supplying its war machine. Then, in 1570, the Pope finally excommunicated Queen Elizabeth and her subjects. We were all infidels now and Britain and the East began to trade.

This Captain had been brought up in Istanbul. His mind was made of minarets and domes. He capped himself with spacious ease. He was his own call to prayer.

'Be confident,' he advised me. 'Be confident even in your mistakes. In Allah there is no wrong road. There is only the road you must travel.'

'And if the road leads nowhere?'

He shrugged. 'Turn your Nowhere into Somewhere.'

He smiled. 'You are young. You have hopes and fears but no experience. You do not know that the gilded palaces and the souks do not really exist. And that is how it should be. You will live in this world as though it is real, until it is no longer real, and then you will know, as I do, that all your adventures and all your possessions, and all your losses, and what you have loved – this gold, this bread, the green glass sea – were things you dreamed as surely as you dreamed of buffalo and watercress.'

'Am I always sleeping?'

'Neither sleeping nor waking. Only the body sleeps and wakes. The mind moves through itself.'

'And when I am dead?'

'Only the body lives and dies.'

He threw his chicken carcass into the sea.

An animal hides to save itself. While the Captain pissed extravagantly overboard, I pleaded sea-sickness and squatted behind a coil of rope.

I know about disguise. I disguise myself from predators. I disguise myself from circumstance. The camouflages I use are elaborate, but I know what they are. Even my body is in disguise today.

But what if my body is the disguise? What if skin, bone, liver, veins, are the things I use to hide myself? I have put them on and I can't take them off. Does that trap me or free me?

'Ali!'

It was the Captain.

'Let me tell you the story of Antioch . . .'

'No one who visits Antioch today can imagine a time when men read in the pink marble libraries, and argued the limits of existence by the fountains in the square.

'And yet it was so.

'No one, riding his donkey through the red dust of the wind-crumbled rocks, can imagine a time when women here bathed in pools as deep as light and freshwater fish criss-crossed in the shadows of the aqueduct.

'Yet it was so.

'Sometimes, travelling through valleys so desolate that a hawk can hardly live, I have seen ships of red porphyry from Egypt and a stone sarcophagus now used by herders for their goats. Saddest of all is the desert of Pisidian Antioch, once the site of a city of commerce and learning, now not even a graveyard.

'Antioch was an aqueduct city. Its stone arches defeated hill and plain alike to draw water from a distant rock tunnel. This sparkling life was carried back to itself and poured over its crops and its citizens until both flourished. They say that the waters of Antioch could cure a blind man and tempt a virgin. Palms were taller than towers.

'It was so.

'A civilisation built on an aqueduct is a perilous one. While its people eat and drink, read and argue, someone must defend the life-giving archway. If they fail, and if they sleep, one barbarian with a pickaxe can drought thought.

'Nobody thinks without a cup of water. The dreams of the dying cannot be irrigated. The world ends, and you with it, to retreat back into the mind of God.

'The barbarians broke up the marble streets and used the slabs for sheepfolds. Shining pillars brought in ships, and dragged by oxen for the magnificence of the temple, were pulled down to be inserted horizontally as wall supports. Birds nested in the dry cups of the public fountains. The barbarians pitched their tents and scooped up the water in their hands. That was enough for them. That was why they had come.

'In the broken aqueduct of Antioch is the history of the downfall of Ephesus, of Miletus, of Pergamum, and of other proud cities of Asia Minor, which once shone among the great names of the world.'

I said, 'Who were the barbarians?'

The Captain said, 'You. The Turks destroyed the aqueduct to Antioch.'

I was angry. I said, 'The Turks are not barbarians.'

He looked at me keenly. 'There is always a city. There is always a civilisation. There is always a barbarian with a pickaxe. Sometimes you are the city, sometimes you are the civilisation, but to become that city, that civilisation, you once took a pickaxe and destroyed what you hated, and what you hated was what you did not understand.

'Antioch was commerce, refinement, leisure, fastidiousness, ideas. Its citizens dressed in silks when we Turks could barely sew a goatskin. What were their libraries and temples to us?

'And now Istanbul is wealthier than Venice and Allah trades across the world. We give our children rubies to play with and the shutters of the seraglios are lined with gold.'

'We are invincible,' I said.

'Do you think so?' he said. 'In three hundred years the Turk may be back among his goats.'

'Impossible!' I cried. 'And if, as you say, nothing exists, then there can be no such place as the future.' (I was pleased with myself for saying this.)

The Captain laughed and kicked me fondly. 'There will be a future. We believe in our unreality too strongly to give it up.'

I was silent. The Captain's kick had dislodged me, and my own unreality was beginning to press on me. I longed to scratch.

'Life is a blessing, Ali, but death is a chance.'

How could Ali barter philosophies when his bulbs were itching? He would gladly have sacrificed the vaporous universe for a chance to get both hands down his trousers, and that is exactly what he was doing when the pirates from Genoa swarmed over the ship.

These men were as burnt as bread in the fire, though their eyes were clear as fire. They murdered the crew, beheaded the Captain, and were about to squeeze Ali like a pomegranate, when one of them noticed his hands clutching his bulbs – that is, his balls.

'Pissing yourself are you?' said the chief pirate.

Ali was so scared that he just told the truth.

'Protecting my treasure,' he said, and his reply was so stupid that it made the pirate laugh. He pulled out his own cock and held it under Ali's nose.

'This is treasure. You aren't worth a flea's ransom.'

Ali sucked it. What else could he do? He had never done it before, but desperation is a good teacher and he soon found his tongue as fluent as any whore's in the marketplace.

The pirate grunted.

'Why kill you when we could sell you?'

And that is how Ali found himself in the apartments of the Italian envoy to the Turks.

Trembling, hungry, dirty and alone, Ali sat on the floor and wondered what would become of him. Two servants entered. One filled a copper bath, while the other laid out food and fresh clothes. Neither spoke to Ali until they had finished their tasks. Then one said, 'You are to eat and bathe and dress yourself and be ready at sundown.'

'Ready for what?'

'The Princess.'

I unstrapped myself and lay in the bath. I reckoned I should make a clean breast of it, though my breasts were not the part in dispute. As a woman, what would be my fate? Mercy or death?

As a boy, I had nothing to look forward to, except perhaps . . .

'Sexual congress,' said the Princess.

She was walking round and round me as though I were a fountain, pausing now and then to dabble her hands. She was beautiful, young, haughty.

'I am to be married in one month, and my husband wishes me to learn something of the arts of love. He has appointed you to teach me.'

'I know nothing,' I said.

'That is why you have been chosen. You are only a boy and can do me neither hurt nor insult. You will be gentle. You will be slow. If I do not like you I shall behead you.'

'Yourself?'

'Of course not.'

'Lady,' I said, 'there must be many in your kingdom better equipped than I am.'

'They have not your treasure,' she said. 'We have heard how you feared less for your life than for your member.'

'My treasure is not what you think it is.'

'I think nothing. Kiss me.'

I kissed her. It wasn't so bad.

Days and nights passed. I kissed her mouth and her neck. I kissed her breasts and her belly. I kissed her lower than her belly and was pleased with the ripples of pleasure I found there. She was dainty and sweet, a dish of figs in fine weather.

We were approaching the inevitable, but we weren't there yet.

Days and nights. Days and nights connected by rivets of pleasure.

Our furnace of love heated time and welded together the separateness of the hours, so that time became what the prophet says it is – continuous, unbroken.

To me, these days will never end. I am always there, in that room with her, or if not I, the imprint of myself – my fossil-love and you discover it.

'Take off your trousers and let me see you.'

So this was the moment. All would be revealed. I no longer cared. Come death, come life, there is a part to play and that is all.

Hesitatingly, I let down the blue and gold of my trousers. There was a silence. Then the Princess said . . .

'I have never seen a man before.'

(You're not seeing one now.)

'The stories I have heard . . . the fleshiness, the swelling . . . but you are like a flower.'

(This was true.)

She touched my bulbs.

'They are like sweet chestnuts.'

(Tulips, my darling, tulips.)

She stroked the waxy coating I kept fresh to protect them. The tips of her fingers glistened.

'What do you call these?'

'This one is Key of Pleasure, and this one is Lover's Dream.' I said this quite sincerely because it was so.

'And what do you call this?'

Her fingers had reached the centre now. I had to think fast.

'I call it my Stem of Spring.'

She laughed delightedly and kissed the red flower, its petals fastened tight into a head. Fortunately my mother had made it quite secure and the Princess could play with it all she liked.

Then a strange thing began to happen. As the Princess kissed and petted my tulip, my own sensations grew exquisite, but as yet no stronger than my astonishment, as I felt my disguise come to life. The tulip began to stand.

I looked down. There it was, making a bridge from my body to hers.

I was still wearing my tunic and the Princess could not see the leather belt that carried everything with it. All she could see, all she could feel, was the eagerness of my bulbs and stem.

I kneeled down, the tulip waving at me as it had done on the hillside that afternoon I cut it down.

Very gently the Princess lowered herself across my knees and I felt the firm red head and pale shaft plant itself in her body. A delicate green-tinted sap dribbled down her brown thighs.

All afternoon I fucked her.

terrible thing to do to a flower . . .

Night. I'm sitting at my screen. There's an e-mail for me. I unwrap it. It says —

That was a terrible thing to do to a flower.

I tap back, 'When you came on-line you said you wanted to be transformed.'
    'Into a flower-fucking Princess?'
    'Well, your alias is Tulip.'
    'That wasn't my idea of romance.'
    'Was it romance you wanted?'
    'Doesn't everyone?'
    'Download *Romeo and Juliet.*'
    'Teenage sex.'
    '*Wuthering Heights.*'
    'The weather's awful and I hate the clothes.'
    '*Heat and Dust.*'
    'I'm allergic to dust.'

'*The Passion.*'

'Never heard of it.'

'Oh well . . .'

'Come on, this is your job. You say you write stories. Write me a story.'

'Freedom just for one night, you said.'

'Yes.'

'All right, but if I start this story . . .'

'Yes?'

'It may change under my hands.'

The screen was dimming. The air was heavy. You and I, separated by distance, intimate of thought, waited. What were we waiting for – fingers resting lightly on the board like a couple of table-turners?

You said, 'Who are you?'

'Call me Ali.'

'Is that your real name?'

'Real enough.'

'Male or female?'

'Does it matter?'

'It's a co-ordinate.'

'This is a virtual world.'

'OK, OK – but just for the record – male or female?'

'Ask the Princess.'

'That was just a story.'

'This is just a story.'

'I call this a true story.'

'How do you know?'

'I know because I'm in it.'

'We're in it together now.'

There was a pause – then I tapped out, 'Let's start. What colour hair do you want?'

'Red. I've always wanted red hair.'

'The same colour as your tulip?'

'Look what happened to that.'

'Don't panic. This is a different disguise.'

'So what shall I wear?'

'It's up to you. Combat or Prada?'

'How much can I spend on clothes?'

'How about $1000?'

'My whole wardrobe or just one outfit?'

'Are you doing this story on a budget?'

'You're the writer.'

'It's your story.'

'What happened to the omniscient author?'

'Gone interactive.'

'Look ... I know this was my idea, but maybe we should quit.'

'What's the problem? This is art not telephone sex.'

'I know, and I said I wanted the freedom to be somebody else – just for one night.'

'So let's do it.'

'I have an early start tomorrow. I should wash my hair. I really think . . .'

'It's too late.'

'What do you mean, it's too late?'

'We've started. We're here.'

'But where are we?'

'You tell me. Where are we?'

'Paris. We're in Paris. There's the Eiffel Tower.'

'Yes, I can see it too. It's evening, the sun's going down . . .'

'And we're in Paris . . .'

NEW DOCUMENT

We were walking together on the broad cobbled path that banks along the Seine. Behind us, the Friday-night cars were queuing in a wrapper of brake lights and exhaust haze; the toxic red of hometime.

On the path as we walked, your sweater tied round your shoulders, compact joggers, moving faster, swerved to avoid us, while lovers, moving slower, stopped in our way, paused to light each other's cigarettes or to kiss.

We were not lovers.

Then.

The evening was stretching itself. The day's muscle had begun to relax. A girl in Lycra fixed her date for the night on her mobile phone. A man in a trenchcoat let his phone ring and ring, smiling to everyone as they glanced at his briefcase going off like an alarm.

At the boat quays couples were waiting to join one of the neon-lit dinner and dance boats, while on other boats – the barges – a cat washed itself by a smoking funnel and a woman with her hair in a scarf threw coffee into the water.

So many lives, and ours too, tangled up with this night, these strangers. Strangers ourselves.

Slightest accidents open up new worlds.

We were both staying at the same hotel. We had arrived the day before, and in the lobby our partners had suddenly spotted one another and thrown their arms around each other like they were old friends. Not surprising, because they were old friends.

You and I had never met. We hung back smiling shyly, slightly irritated by all this bonhomie we couldn't share. Then the plan had been made for the next night, to eat at a restaurant nearby, and would it matter – no, it would be fun – if those two long-lost buddies went on ahead, and you and I walked to the restaurant together, getting to know each other.

Simple. Easy.

Yes.

Not knowing you, and knowing that small talk is not my best point, I started to tell you about George Mallory, the Everest mountaineer. I'm putting him in a book I'm writing, and strangers often like to hear how writers write their books. It saves the bother of reading them.

'So you're a writer?'

'Yes.'

'I've never heard of you.'

'No.'

'Have you had anything published?'

'Yes.'

'Can I buy it in the shops?'

'Yes.'

'What, here in Paris?'

'Yes.'

'In French?'

'Yes.'

'In English too?'

'Yes.'

'Oh really?'

(I said small talk is not my best point.)

'So you're a writer?'

'Yes.'

'What kind of things do you write?'

'Fiction, mostly.'

'Stuff you make up?'

'Yes.'

'I prefer real life.'

'Why is that?'

'No surprises.'

'Don't you like surprises?'

'Not since my fifth birthday when I was given an exploding cake.'

'Could you eat it?'

'The candles were little sticks of dynamite and they blew the cream and sponge all over the room.'

'What did you do?'

'Scraped it off the walls. Tried to act normal.'

'Difficult . . .'

'Oh yes.'

(Then she paused. Then she said . . .) 'To me that's life – a cake with little sticks of dynamite on the top.'

'That doesn't sound like a life with no surprises.'

'Oh, but it is. That's just what it is. You see, I know it's going to blow up in my face.'

I looked sideways at her as we walked. To me she seemed confident and poised in soft black jeans, white shirt, a slash of lipstick, and a handbag built to take a credit card and a make-up brush. Her sweater was a ribbed cashmere crewneck, tied like a sack, hanging like a dancer.

Simple.

Expensive.

'What brings you to Paris?' (Small talk, not bad.)

'The Eiffel Tower.'

'Do you like towers?'

'I like structures without cladding.'

'OK, it's a good motto.'

'I try to let the lines show through. Not on my face, of course, but elsewhere. My work, my life, my body.'

(Suddenly, very badly, I wanted to see her body. I suppressed the thought.)

'Clean living?' I said.

'Hardly.'

'What then?'

'Clear space. The easiest thing in the world is to wallpaper yourself from head to foot and put an armchair in your stomach.'

'Sounds uncomfortable.'

'Oh no, it's very comfortable. That's why people do it.'

'But not you.'

(She suddenly took my hand.) 'This is where I feel things.'

(She guided my hand over the low waistband of her jeans.) 'Excitement, danger . . .'

(She flattened my hand on her abdomen and held it there.)

'Sex. And to go on feeling I have to keep some empty space.'

(Suddenly she let my hand drop. I looked at it sadly.)

She said, 'What about you? What brings you to Paris?'

'A story I'm writing.'

'Is it about Paris?'

'No, but Paris is in it.'

'What is it about?'

'Boundaries. Desire.'

'What are your other books about?'

'Boundaries. Desire.'

'Can't you write about something else?'

'No.'

'So why come to Paris?'

'Another city. Another disguise.'

We went up on to a little wooden bridge and lounged against the metal rail. The broad view of the river was a cine film of the weekend, with its amateur, hand-held feel of lovers and dogs and electric light and the spontaneous, unsteady movement of people crossing this way and that, changing their minds, pausing, going out of focus, looming too close. The ribbon of film that was the moving river fluttered and unrolled and projected itself against the open sky and the jostle of the Ile de la Cité.

Frame by frame, that Friday night was shot and exposed and thrown away, carried by the river, by time, canned up only in memory, but in itself, scene by scene, perfect.

I thought, 'This is all I have, all I can be sure of. The rest is gone. The rest may not follow.'

There was a woman near me, eating an ice cream with the intensity of a sacrament. The look on her face, her concentration, belonged to the altar.

A man knelt down and fastened his Scottie dog into a little tartan coat. Feet passed round him. His fingers fumbled with the buckles.

A child, holding its mother's hand, was crying over a punctured Mickey Mouse balloon and then, the limping, failing helium ears and deflating black nose lurched over the railing and slipped down flat on the water.

Away it went – mouse, dog, ice cream, now. Already we were in another now, and the pink of the sky had faded.

'Where's the restaurant?' you said.

'I don't know. I thought you knew.'

'No – I thought you knew.'

'Well, what was the name?'

'Ali's. A Turkish place.'

'Are you sure?'

'We can call the hotel. The concierge will know.'

'We're going to be late.'

'There's plenty of time.'

She smiled and rested her arm around my shoulders. I tried to look natural.

'Are you usually so friendly with strangers?'

'Always.'

'Any particular reason?'

'A stranger is a safe place. You can tell a stranger anything.'

'Suppose I put it in my book?'

'You write fiction.'

'So?'

'So you won't lash me to the facts.'

'But I might tell the truth.'

'Facts never tell the truth. Even the simplest facts are misleading.'

'Like the times of the trains.'

'And how many lovers you've had.'

I looked at her curiously. Where was this leading?

'How many have you had?'

'9.48,' she said, sounding like a platform announcement.

'Was that the previous one or the one here now?'

'The one here now is not listed in the timetable.'

'What does that mean?'

'It means I'm married, but not to him.'

'Then to whom?'

'Oh, to a man built like a dining car – solid, welcoming, always about to serve lunch.'

'Don't you like that?'

'There are nights when I'd prefer a couchette.'

'Is that why you're in Paris?'

'And there are nights when I'd prefer nothing at all.'

'A structure without cladding.'

'As you get older, the open spaces start to close up.'

'You seem to have slipped through.'

'I get reckless. I risk more than I should.'

'Have you left your husband?'

'No, just lied to him.'

'Can you lie to someone you love?'

'It's kinder than telling the truth.'

'Are you still close?'

'As close as two people growing apart can be.'

She walked ahead, her sweater swinging against her back. Then she turned to me.

'You keep the form and the habit of what you have, but gradually you empty it of meaning.'

'If you feel like that, you should leave.'

'I still love him.'

'You can love someone and leave them. Sometimes you should.'

'Not me.'

'Well, anyway, it's not my business.'

Then she made a speech. I suppose you can guess the lines.

Inside her marriage there were too many clocks and not enough time. Too much furniture and too little space. Outside her marriage, there would be nothing to hold her, nothing to shape her. The space she found would be outer space. Space without gravity or weight, where bit by bit the self disintegrates.

'Can't you understand that?'

'Yes.'

'But?'

I didn't answer. I had heard these arguments before. I had used them myself. They tell some truth, but not all the truth, and the truth they deny is a truth about the heart. The body can endure compromise and the mind can be seduced by it. Only the heart protests.

The heart. Carbon-based primitive in a silicon world.

'There's something wrong.'

'With what I say?'

'With the sweet reasonableness of it all.'

'You want me to storm out with nothing but a tapestry and a pair of candlesticks?'

'I wasn't thinking about your luggage.'

'A friend I knew did just that. Took nothing else and left.'

'I admire her.'

'You are an absolutist then.'

'What's one of those?'

'All or nothing.'

'What else is there?'

'The middle ground. Ever been there?'

'I've seen it on the map.'

'You should take a trip.'

'And when I get there I can go round and round in circles like everyone else.'

'What have I done to deserve this?'

'You're the one who talked about risk and freedom and structure without cladding.'

'Meaning?'

'Meaning you just want what everybody wants – everything.'

'What's wrong with that?'

'Nothing – but you have to pay for it yourself.'

'So I want to have my cake and eat it?'

'That's understandable, given your history.'

She laughed and took my arm, holding me to her.

'I like you.'

'Why?'

'You want to fight.'

'The world is my boxing ring.'

'Do you have to fight everyone?'

'Only the enemy.'

'Is it that simple?'

'You can be so subtle you just tie yourself up in knots.'

'You can be so simple you just go nine rounds with yourself.'

'Well yes, I do, often.'

'What for?'

'To stay on my toes.'

'You should relax.'

'I look silly in an armchair.'

'What do you look like in bed?'

I was so surprised I said nothing. Then, on the bridge, not caring about anyone else, she leaned forward and kissed me. A soft open kiss.

'This is a bad idea.'
    'Why?'
    'You are married to one person, in Paris with another, and we're late for supper.'
    'You only live once.'
    'You can live as many times as you like at your own expense.'
    'So you won't buy me supper then?'

She was laughing. She laughed at my discomfort, at my seriousness. That's how I remember her, laughing at me, on a wooden bridge in Paris.

She had been laughing that afternoon when we were caught in the rain at Les Halles. I had been out on my own, looking for a particular shop where I could buy a snare. I didn't realise it would be set for me.

    The shop – Exterminateur des Animaux Nuisibles – has been in the old meat market since the 1920s, and its wood and glass shopfront, and its high-polished counter, have never changed. The customer can brood over the cockroach chart and buy a *nasse* or a *piège* that will kill almost anything. The shop-keepers serve with the solemnity of bank clerks. Their business is hushed and discreet. Your purchase is wrapped in brown paper and tied with string. When I was there, a man in a brown overall was testing a mousetrap with a piece of Roquefort.

As I came out, you sprang at me, laughing, and caught my arm to drag me away. You said something about a string quartet in the Metro. The rain was coming down in slices. A beggar with a shredded umbrella wanted a franc.

We ran.

We ran past a group of men – button-down shirts, cardigans, cigarettes – sheltering under an awning while the rain pelted off the canvas and on to the tips of their shoes.

We ran through the scattering shoppers, through the boys on bicycles, through the wicker chairs hurled indoors by the barman.

We ran through the jump-course of fake Louis Vuitton luggage, vanishing under a tarpaulin to the yells of the African sellers. We ran straight for the steaming Metro and into a cascade of Vivaldi.

Four kids – and kids is all they were – had set up their music stands and opened their instrument cases, and they played without hesitation, passionately, blocking the entrances and exits, and nobody cared because the music was stronger than either the need to go home or the flooded afternoon.

You were delighted. Your hair dripped on to your shoulders and your mouth was slightly open. Your face was flushed from the running and the rain. I thought you were lovely, and I smiled too, at the pleasure of it, and at the chance.

I had planned my afternoon. Chance had changed it. Is chance the snare or what breaks the snare?

We caught a train to the Louvre. You wanted to come up through the great glass pyramid. You said it was like being reborn. You said it made you feel like an Egyptian Princess, and for a moment I thought I knew you, by the waters at Karnak, and I caught the scent of your herb-anointed bandages, and the smell of your fear, as they carried you into the darkness from which there can be no return.

But there you were, running up the staircase, round and round, from the basement of yourself, free at last, and as you burst into the steel and glass of the pyramid, the sun came out, turning the puddles into ten thousand mirrors that shone on the glass as if to furnace it.

Nothing is solid. Nothing is fixed. These are images that time changes and that change time, just as the sun and the rain play on the surface of things.

'Champagne?'

You pointed to the Café Marly, and we walked across to a glittering table. A waiter in a white jacket brushed the raindrops off the marble surface, and flared his nostrils at us with that hotel-trade mixture of servility and disgust.

'*Deux coupes de champagne.*'

He nodded his head as though he were snapping it shut. Around us, underneath the statues of dead Frenchmen, teenagers shoved postcards into their backpacks and drank Coke from the bottle. The sun was sharp. Everybody was happy. I was happy with the lightness of being in a foreign city and the relief from identity it brings. I stretched out my legs. I stretched out my mind. My mind reached forward into the unlimited space it can occupy when I loose it from its kennel.

The waiter returned with his silver tray and put down the two flutes with a little click. You raised your glass.

'Well, what shall we drink to?'

'Chance.'

'Here's to Chance.'

'Now you choose.'

She paused and thought a moment, then smiled.

'All right. Harold Bloom.'

'Harold Bloom?'

'For his translation of the Jewish blessing. I guess you're not Jewish?'

I shook my head. She raised her glass again.

'More life into a time without boundaries.'

Then something like a raindrop was in her eye.

The evening was cooling. She and I had walked without speaking, back over the Pont Neuf, to a little triangle of grass and birch trees set on all sides with small restaurants. I like to eat here.

Someone once called it 'the sex of Paris'.

I was angry with myself. The afternoon had been an antici-pation — I don't know what for — I do know what for, but I would have been glad and disappointed if nothing had started to happen. If we had gone to the restaurant as planned, and the rest had stayed as a memory whose truthfulness is not in the detail.

The trouble is that in imagination anything can be perfect. Downloaded into real life, it was messy. She was messy. I was messy. I blamed myself. I had wanted to be caught.

We slowed down. She spoke.

'You're angry with me.'

'This is the place — Paul's.'

'I said too much too soon.'

'The décor hasn't changed since the 1930s.'

'I don't hold you cheap.'

'The women who serve wear white aprons and won't speak English.'

'I just want to hold you.'

She took me in her arms and I was so angry I could have struck her, and at the bottom of my anger, conducting it, was a copper coil of desire.

'And I want to kiss you.'

A man was exercising two Dalmatians under the trees. Spots

ran in front of my eyes.

'Kiss you here and here.'

The man threw them two red tennis balls and the dogs ran for the balls and fetched them back – black and white and red, black and white and red.

This feels like a grainy movie – the black dresses and white aprons of the matrons moving inside the lighted window of Paul's. Your black jeans and white shirt. The night wrapping round you like a sweater. Your arms wrapped round me. Two Dalmatians.

Yes, this is black and white. The outlines are clear. I must turn away. Why don't I?

In my mouth there is a red ball of desire.

'These tiny hairs on your neck . . .'

Fetch. My heart returns to me what I turn away. I am my own master but not always master of myself. This woman wants to be . . .

'Your lover.'

We went inside. I ordered artichoke vinaigrette and slices of duck with *haricots verts*. You had pea soup and smoked eel. I could have done with several bottles of wine, but settled for a Paris goblet, at one gulp, from the house carafe.

You tore up the bread with nervous fingers.

'Where were we?'

'It's not where I want to be.'

'It didn't feel like that when I held you.'

'No, you're right.'

'Well then?'

She has beautiful hands, I thought, watching her origami the baguette. Beautiful hands – deft, light, practical, practised. Mine was not the first body and it wouldn't be the last. She popped the bread into her mouth.

'Where shall I start?' I said, ready with my defence.

'Not at the beginning,' she said, feeding me crumbs.

'Why not?'

'We both know the usual reasons, the unwritten rules. No need to repeat them.'

'You really don't care, do you?'

'About you? Yes.'

'About the mess this will make.'

'I'm not a Virgo.'

'I am.'

'Oh God, just my luck. I bet you're obsessed with the laundry.'

'I am, as it happens.'

'Oh yes, I had a Virgo once. He could never leave the washing machine alone. Day and night, wash, wash, wash. I used to call him Lady Macbeth.'

'What are you going to call me?'

'I'll think of something.'

The artichoke arrived and I began to peel it away, fold by fold, layer by layer, dipping it. There is no secret about eating artichoke, or what the act resembles. Nothing else gives itself up so satisfyingly towards its centre. Nothing else promises and rewards. The tiny hairs are part of the pleasure.

What should I have eaten? Beetroot, I suppose.

A friend once warned me never to consider taking as a lover anyone who disliked either artichokes or champagne. That was good advice, but better advice might have been never to order artichokes or champagne with someone who should not be your lover.

At least I had chosen plain red wine.

And then I remembered the afternoon.

She looked at me, smiling, her lips glossy with oil.

'What are you thinking about?'

'This afternoon.'

'We should have gone to bed then.'

'We hardly spoke six sentences to each other.'

'That's the best way. Before the complications start.'

'Don't worry. No start. No complications.'
'Are you always such a moralist?'
'You make me sound like a Jehovah's Witness.'
'You can doorstep me any night.'
'Will you stop it?'
'As you say, we haven't started yet.'
'After supper we go back to the hotel and say goodnight.'
'And tomorrow you will catch the Eurostar to London.'
'And the day after you'll fly Air France to New York.'
'You must be a Jehovah's Witness.'
'Why must I?'
'You're not married but you won't sleep with me.'
'You are married.'
'That's my problem.'
'True . . .'
'Well then . . .'
'I've done it before and it became my problem.'
'What happened?'
'I fell in love.'

It was a long time ago. It feels like another life until I remember it was my life, like a letter you turn up in your own handwriting, hardly believing what it says.

I loved a woman who was married. She loved me too, and if there had been less love or less marriage I might have escaped. Perhaps no one really does escape.

She wanted me because I was a pool where she drank. I wanted her because she was a lover and a mother all mixed up into one. I wanted her because she was as beautiful as a warm afternoon with the sun on the rocks.

The damage done was colossal.

'You lost her?'
     'Of course I did.'
     'Have you got over it?'
     'It was a love affair not an assault course.'
     'Love is an assault course.'
     'Some wounds never heal.'
     'I'm sorry.'

She held out her hand. What a strange world it is where you can have as much sex as you like but love is taboo. I'm talking about the real thing, the grand passion, which may not allow affection or convenience or happiness. The truth is that love smashes into your life like an ice floe, and even if your heart is built like the *Titanic* you go down. That's the size of it, the immensity of it. It's not proper, it's not clean, it's not containable.

She held out her hand. 'You're still angry.'
     'I'm still alive.'

What to say? That the end of love is a haunting. A haunting of dreams. A haunting of silence. Haunted by ghosts it is easy to become a ghost. Life ebbs. The pulse is too faint. Nothing stirs you. Some people approve of this and call it healing. It is not healing. A dead body feels no pain.

'But pain is pointless.'
  'Not always.'
  'Then what is the use of suffering? Can you tell me that?'

She thinks I'm holding on to pain. She thinks the pain is a souvenir. Perhaps she thinks that pain is the only way I can feel. As it is, the pain reminds me that my feelings are damaged. The pain doesn't stop me loving – only a false healing could do that – the pain tells me that neither my receptors nor my transmitters are in perfect working order. The pain is not feeling, but it has become an instrument of feeling.

She said, 'Do you still like having sex?'
  'You talk as though I've had an amputation.'
  'I think you have. I think someone has cut out your heart.'

I looked at her and my eyes were clear.

'That's not how the story ends.'

Stop.

There is always the danger of automatic writing. The danger of writing yourself towards an ending that need never be told. At a certain point the story gathers momentum. It convinces itself, and does its best to convince you, that the end in sight is the only possible outcome. There is a fatefulness and a loss of control that are somehow comforting. This was your script, but now it writes itself.

Stop.

Break the narrative. Refuse all the stories that have been told so far (because that is what the momentum really is), and try to tell the story differently – in a different style, with different weights – and allow some air to those elements choked with centuries of use, and give some substance to the floating world.

In quantum reality there are millions of possible worlds, unactualised, potential, perhaps bearing in on us, but only reachable by wormholes we can never find. If we do find one, we don't come back.

In those other worlds events may track our own, but the ending will be different. Sometimes we need a different ending.

I can't take my body through space and time, but I can send my mind, and use the stories, written and unwritten, to tumble me out in a place not yet existing – my future.

The stories are maps. Maps of journeys that have been made and might have been made. A Marco Polo route through territory real and imagined.

Some of the territory has become as familiar as a seaside resort. When we go there we know we will build sandcastles and get sunburnt and that the café menu never changes.

Some of the territory is wilder and reports do not tally. The guides are only good for so much. In these wild places I become part of the map, part of the story, adding my version to the versions there. This Talmudic layering of story on story, map on map, multiplies possibilities but also warns me of the weight of accumulation. I live in one world – material, seeming-solid – and the weight of that is quite enough. The other worlds I can reach need to keep their lightness and their speed of light. What I carry back from those worlds to my world is another chance.

She put out her hand. 'I want to rescue you.'
　　'From what?'
　　'From the past. From pain.'
　　'The past is only a way of talking.'
　　'Then from pain.'
　　'I don't want a wipe-clean life.'
　　'Don't be so prickly.'
　　'I'm sorry.'
　　'What do you want? Tell me.'
　　'No compromises.'
　　'That's impossible.'
　　'Only the impossible is worth the effort.'

'Are you a fanatic or an idealist?'

'Why do you need to label me?'

'I need to understand.'

'No, you want to explain me to yourself. You're not sure, so you need a label. But I'm not a piece of furniture with the price on the back.'

'This is a heavy way to get some sex.'

The waitress cleared the plates and brought us some brown and yellow banded ice cream, the same colour as the ceilings and walls. It even had the varnishy look of the 1930s. The cherries round the edges were like Garbo kisses. You speared one and fed it to me.

'Come to bed with me.'

'Now?'

'Yes now. It's all I can offer. It's all I can ask.'

'No difficulties, no complications?'

'None.'

'Except that someone will be waiting for you in Room 29.'

'He'll be drunk and fast asleep.'

'And someone will be waiting for me.'

'Someone special?'

'Just a friend.'

'Well then . . .'

'Good manners?'

'I'll leave a message at the night desk.'

She got up and fiddled with some change for the phone.

'Wait . . .'

She didn't answer. There she was, at the phone, her face turned away from me.

We went to a small hotel that used to be a spa.

The bathrooms still have steam vents and needle showers, and if you turn the wrong knob while you're cleaning your teeth the whole bedroom will fill up with steam like the set of a Hitchcock movie. From somewhere out of the steam the phone will ring. There will be a footstep on the landing, voices. Meanwhile you'll be stumbling for the window, naked, blinded, with only a toothbrush between yourself and Paris.

The room we took at the Hotel Tonic was on the top floor. It had three beds with candlewick counterpanes and a view over the rooftops of the street. Opposite us, cut into the frame of the window, was a boy dancing alone to a Tina Turner record. We leaned out against the metal safety bars, watching him, watching the cars pull away. You put your hand on the small of my back under my shirt.

This is how we made love.

You kissed my throat.

The boy was dancing.

You kissed my collarbone.

Two taxi drivers were arguing in the street.
You put your tongue into the channel of my breasts.
A door slammed underneath us.
I opened your legs on to my hip.
Two pigeons were asleep under the red wings of the roof.
You began to move with me – hands, tongue, body.
Game-show laughter from the television next door.
You took my breasts in both hands and I slid you out of your
jeans.
Rattle of bottles on a tray.
You don't wear knickers.
A door opened. The tray was set down.
You keep your breasts in a black mesh cage.
Car headlights reflected in the dressing-table mirror.
Lie down with me.
Get on top of me.
Ease yourself, just there, just there . . .
Harry speaks French, he'll pick up the beer.
Push.
Stella or Bud?
Harder.
Do you want nuts?
Make me come. Make me.
Ring her after midnight your time, she said.
Just fuck me.
Got the number?

Fuck me.

The next morning I woke late and turned over to kiss her.

She had gone. The sheet was still warm but she had gone. I lay there, my growing agitation of mind beginning to fight with the gentle heaviness of my body. I had no idea what to do, so I did the obvious – got dressed and ran round the corner to our other hotel.

At the Relais de Louvre my own room was empty. Not surprising. There were my clothes and travel bag, and one ticket home. Well, I had given up any right to company.

I went down the corridor to Room 29. The door was open. The maid was cleaning up.

'*Où est la Mademoiselle?*'

The maid shrugged and switched on her Hoover. Paris is full of mademoiselles.

I rang the front desk.

Rien.

Room 29 had checked out and there was no forwarding address.

I walked to a little café on the river and ordered some coffee and croissants. No difficulties. No complications. Not even goodbye. So that's the end of it then.

I felt as if I had blundered into someone else's life by chance, discovered I wanted to stay, then blundered back into my own, without a clue, a hint, or a way of finishing the story.

Who was I last night? Who was she?

virtual world

Night.

I logged on to the Net. There were no e-mails for me. You had run out on the story. Run out on me. Vanished.

I typed in your address.

Nothing.

I set one of the search engines to find you.

Nothing.

Here I am like a penitent in a confessional. I want to tell you how I feel, but there's nobody on the other side of the screen.

What did I expect?

This is a virtual world. This is a world inventing itself. Daily, new landmasses form and then submerge. New continents of thought break off from the mainland. Some benefit from a trade wind, some sink without trace. Others are like Atlantis – fabulous, talked about, but never found.

Found objects wash up on the shores of my computer. Tin cans and old tyres mix with the pirate's stuff. The buried treasure is really there, but caulked and outlandish. Hard to spot because unfamiliar, and few of us can see what has never been named.

I'm looking for something, it's true.

I'm looking for the meaning inside the data.

That's why I trawl my screen like a beachcomber – looking for you, looking for me, trying to see through the disguise. I guess I've been looking for us both all my life.

SEARCH

It began with a promise:

'While I am living I shall rescue you.'

That dark night I took a ladder and propped it against the window where I knew you slept. You would not be sleeping.

The window was barred with iron, and you were like an anchorite behind your grille, and I was more like a penitent than a knight, as I whispered to you and touched your fingers. You said you would rather have me with you that night than see the sun rise on another day.

You were sun and moon to me.

I took the iron bars in my hands and tore them out of the stone, and though I cut my hand through to the bone I never felt it, but came to you and lay with you in the darkness, in the silence, your body as white and soft as moonlight.

In the morning, when I had long since gone, and you slept late, your servant drew back the bed curtains and saw the sheets and pillows soaked in blood. It was soon known that someone must have been with you in your room and the hissing started.

You were faithless. You were treacherous. You would be burnt.

Many times has your lord and my King, with a heavy heart, committed you to burning. Many times have I rescued you, through combat with your accuser, for the King, who is judge of all, cannot fight for his own wife.

My name is Lancelot.

'Lancelot du Lac,' you said, rowing your body over me.

I was the place where you anchored. I was the deep water where you could be weightless. I was the surface where you saw your own reflection. You scooped me up in your hands.

That you were married to someone else meant nothing to me. Which is more important – a dead marriage or a living love? You never chose private happiness over public duty, you asked only that happiness be there – a view from the window, a crack in the casing – that sometimes you could ease yourself out, unclothe yourself, swim in me.

There was never a time when he called you and you did not answer. You asked – without asking – that when he did not call you, there would be no need to answer.

Then you called for me, and no hawk was swifter to the wrist.

I saved you from the fire, but the fire I could not put out was burning at our feet. Many times have you and I turned away from each other, our faces proud, our hearts seeming cold, and only our feet, which smouldered the clean stone where they trod, betrayed us.

My feet, bare and clean on the cold floor of my penance, left charcoal marks where I walked. The flagstones of your heart have become hearthstones. Wherever we stood, there was a fire at our feet.

'One day this will destroy us,' you said, your lips like tongs, moving the burning parts of me.

But I wondered how it could destroy us when it *was* us? We had become this love. We were not lovers. We were love.

Your marrow is in my bones. My blood is in your veins. Your cock is in my cunt. My breasts weigh under your dress. My fighting arm is sinew'd to your shoulder. Your tiny feet stand my ground. In full armour I am wearing nothing but your shift, and when you plait your hair you wind it round my head. Your eyes are green. Mine are brown. When I see through your green eyes, I see the meadows bright with grass. When you creep behind my retina, you see the flick of trout in the reeds of the lake.

I can hold you up with one hand, but you can balance me

on your fingertips. Last night, angry, you split my lip with your fists, then wept over a scar from a boar.

I am not wounded unless you wound me.

I am not strong unless you are my strength.

Her name is Guinevere.

The rumours increased. There was a plot. Mordred and Agravaine warned the King against us and set to trap me in your room. I killed all twelve of those cowards who lusted after our bravery, and it is brave to love, for love is the mortal enemy of death. Love is death's twin, born in the same moment, each fighting for mastery, and if death takes all, love would do the same. Yet it is easier to die than to love.

Death will shatter me, but in love's service I have been shattered many times.

There was a day, I remember, when I rode after you in full armour and made my horse swim the Thames to find you. At the other side my horse was shot down.

I followed on foot, but my armour was so heavy that I made little progress, and I would have gladly torn off helmet and plates, and thrown my shield away, except that a man cannot even unbuckle his armour by himself.

Exhausted and weary, a man in iron clothes, I came at last to where you were, and killed your captors and set you free.

Then I stretched out my arms like a little child and begged you to uncouple my harness and unlace my metal gloves. I knelt down and you lifted up my visor and kissed me.

My armour off, it lay like an effigy of myself on the floor. I was naked with you, carapace of hero put aside. I was not Lancelot. I was your lover.

Why then fear death, which cannot enter the body further than you have entered mine?

Why then fear death, which cannot dissolve me more than I dissolve in you, this day, this night, always?

Death will not separate us. Love is as strong as death.

Your death was commanded for the next day.

As the soldiers were tying your hands and packing the dry straw under your bare feet, I rode up on my white mare, and I cared nothing for anyone who fell under my sword. I took you up behind me and carried you to my own castle, and begged you to come with me to France, to my lands, to my heart, for ever.

You would not break your marriage vow.

And then the wars began. The wars that ruined us all.

Most blamed you, some blamed me, but underneath the blaming of our love, hid many other wraths, restless to be vented. What began as good reason became good excuse. The war was pursued long after any advantage for either side.

I was riding through the burnt fields and bloodied streams, looking for you. My horse picked her way with delicate hooves over the bodies of the dead.

I had been told you had entered a nunnery, and I found you there at last. Dismounting from my horse, I walked to the walled garden and looked through the little grille.

You were unaware of me. You were sitting on a low stone bench with your hands in front of you, palms up, as though you were a book you were straining to read. Though you were all in black and I could not see your face, the arch of your back, your shoulders, your neck, made a curve I knew from loving you.

I looked at my own hands that had touched you everywhere, and I took hold of the grille, as I had done before, and I would have torn it out of the wall to get to you, but suddenly you looked up. You saw me. You fainted.

I ran to the Abbess and begged her to allow me into the garden. Reluctantly she did so, for you are still the Queen, and I am still Lancelot, though the meaning of those names has become a noise.

In the garden you had recovered yourself. You were tall, upright, stern. As I approached, you held up your hand, and I would gladly have plucked my heart out of my body to make you hold it as you once held it – the core of me in your hands.

'This love has destroyed us,' you said.

'Not love, but others' envy of it.'

'I had no right to love you,' you said.

'But you did love me and you love me now.'

I took a step forward. She shook her head.

'You will never see me again while I am alive.'

'Let me kiss you.'

She shook her head.

I rode away and my tears made a lake of me, and for seven nights I rode continuously, not knowing where, under desolate cliffs and through exhausted valleys, until I came to a chapel and a hermitage.

I took the robe of hermit on me and did penance there for seven years, and in the seventh year I had a dream three times in one night.

The dream told me to take a funeral bier to Almsbury, where I should find the Queen dead. I was to walk beside her body to Glastonbury and bury her beside her lord and my King.

The next morning I set out and after two days came to my destination. The Queen had died half an hour before, saying to her women that she prayed her eyes would never have the power to see me again while she was alive.

I walked beside her, and it seemed to me that the years had

sprung back and it was May again. The Maytime when I was sent through the forest to bring Guinevere to marry King Arthur.

All that long journey we had talked and sung together, and eaten privately in a jewelled tent. I fell in love with her then, and I have never been able to stop loving her, or to stop my body leaping at the sight of her.

There is no penance that can calm love and no regret that can make it bitter.

You are closed and shuttered to me now, a room without doors or windows, and I cannot enter. But I fell in love with you under the open sky and death cannot change that.

Death can change the body but not the heart.

great and ruinous lovers

The great and ruinous lovers.

Lancelot and Guinevere.
Tristan and Isolde.
Siegfried and Brünnhilde.
Romeo and Juliet.
Cathy and Heathcliffe.
Vita and Violet.
Oscar and Bosie.
Burton and Taylor.
Abelard and Heloïse.
Paolo and Francesca.

There are many more. This is a list you can write yourself. Some are greater than others. Some more ruinous. Some tales have been told many times, others privately and by letter. Love's script has no end of beginnings. The characters and the scenery change.

There are three possible endings: Revenge. Tragedy. Forgiveness.

The stories we sit up late to hear are love stories. It seems that we cannot know enough about this riddle of our lives. We go back and back to the same scenes, the same words, trying to scrape out the meaning. Nothing could be more familiar than love. Nothing else eludes us so completely.

I do not know whether or not science will formulate its grand theory of the universe. I know that it will not make it any easier to read the plain text of our hearts. It is plain but it seems like a secret alphabet. We train as our own Egyptologists, hoping the fragments will tell a tale. We work at night as alchemists, struggling to decipher the letters mirrored and reversed. We are people who trace with our finger a marvellous book, but when we turn to read it again the letters have vanished. Always the book must be rewritten. Sometimes a letter at a time is all we can do.

My search for you, your search for me, is a search after something that cannot be found. Only the impossible is worth the effort. What we seek is love itself, revealed now and again in human form, but pushing us beyond our humanity into animal instinct and god-like success. The love we seek overrules human nature. It has a wildness in it and a glory that we want more than life itself. Love never counts the cost, to itself or others, and nothing is as cruel as love. There is no love that does not pierce the hands and feet.

Merely human love does not satisfy us, though we settle for it. It is an encampment on the edge of the wilderness, and we light the fire and turn up the lamp, and tell stories until late at night of those great loves lost and won.

The wilderness is not tamed. It waits – beautiful and terrible – beyond the reach of the campfire. Now and again someone gets up to leave, forced to read the map of themselves, hoping that the treasure is really there. A record of their journey comes back to us in note form, sometimes just a letter in a dead man's pocket.

Love is worth death. Love is worth life. My search for you, your search for me, goes beyond life and death into one long call in the wilderness. I do not know if what I hear is an answer or an echo. Perhaps I will hear nothing. It doesn't matter. The journey must be made.

open it

Night. The search engines are quiet.

I keep throwing the stories overboard, like a message in a bottle, hoping you'll read them, hoping you'll respond.

You don't respond.

I warned you that the story might change under my hands. I forgot that the storyteller changes too. I was under your hands.

Later, much later, there's a plane ticket on the screen – destination Naples.

Maybe you want an opera not a story.

Maybe, but the story has already gone on ahead. There it is, competing in the waves with the hydrofoils and rich men's yachts. It looks like a plastic bottle but there's something inside.

You thought, didn't you, that you could start something and stop it when you pleased? Pick it up, put it down. A little light reading. A bedtime story.

Freedom just for one night.

The story is reading you now, line by line.
    Do you know what happens next?
    Go on, open it.
    Open it . . .

VIEW

An island of rocks. Sea-bound. Roofed with birds.

The island is like an idea lifted out of the sea's brooding.

The island is an idea of itself – an imaginary island and a real one – real and imaginary reflecting together in the mirror of the water.

Look in the mirror. What can you see?

There's Tiberius hiding from the plots of Empire. There he is, ruler of the ancient world, rowed from Naples in a hundred-oared galley, each stroke of the wood to the stroke of the drum, while flutes soothe him to sleep.

He called Capri a sacred place and decorated its wooded slopes with villas and temples and *nymphaea* and shrines. Nowadays, underneath the tourist trade are the remains of the professional gods. The mosaic of the past is a fragment – a bit of coloured glass, a corner of tile – but the present is no more complete. The paint is fresher, that's all.

From an open boat the tourists crane back their necks to

stare at the Villa Jovis. The rock face is sheer and unclimbable. Far up, the dot of a human appears.

'*Eccola!*' says the guide. 'From that spot Tiberio flung his victims to death. *Morte! Morte! Morte!*'

He spreads his hands expressively, and the party shades its shaded eyes to better imagine the tumbling body twisted through time.

'Women too,' says the guide. '*Tiberio cattivo,*' and he spits.

Of course, it may well be that spiteful Suetonius was a slandermonger. Perhaps Tiberius never did hurl his enemies into space-time. An imaginary island invents itself. It takes part in its own myth. There is something about this place that suggests more than it reveals. Capri has been thoroughly plundered – its woods, its treasures, its stories. It has been well known for more than two thousand years. Yet it slips through the net of knowing as easily as the small fishes in the harbour.

The Marina Grande was built in the nineteenth century to accommodate the smart steamboats bringing the smart English to the smart hotels. Aquatints of the harbour show luggage being piled on to handcarts, much as it is today, and horse and donkey landaus jostling for custom where the taxi rank is.

The funicular railway, completed in 1906, connects the harbour to the main square, and its sheer, vertiginous ascent is a kind of Tiberio-strategy in miniature. If the tension between the upward car and the downward car were to relax, both cars would crash through the red pantile roofs of the side-by-side houses and, collecting olive trees and grapevines as a memorial, the train and its passengers would career into the sea, nose first, broken backed, to join the other wrecks never recovered.

This does not happen. The upward car brakes the downward car, while the downward car powers the upward car. The passengers are aboard. A bell rings, like the start of an exam. The driver, who was lounging Italian-wise drinking a thimble of coffee, flings it aside, dives into his cab and releases the brake.

It is the moment of action for which there is no preparation.

As I stand in the front car, holding on to the rail, and feeling the train move down through the sunlight towards the tunnel, I feel like I am being born. I find myself gripping the bar, unable to take my eyes off the point where the single track divides as it enters the tunnel. It divides into a curved diamond, a vulva, a dark mouth – one of the many caves on the island where a rite of passage is observed.

Then we are out again, into the sunshine, into the bustle of the harbour, with one glance back at the slow car of souls leaving this life.

Then, as now, the pleasantest way from the Marina Grande to the square is to be driven privately, round and round the impossible bends, the driver with one hand on the wheel, the other glued to the horn. He would sooner let go of the wheel than give up hooting.

Everyone prefers the open-top cars, and those drivers not fortunate enough to own a factory model customise their own. They saw off the roof, sometimes leaving the window pillars, sometimes not. Then they rig up an awning out of bamboo, and fasten it to the windscreen at one end and the boot lid at the other with rusty crocodile clips. The kind you use to jump-start a flat battery.

These bamboo cars will carry anything for you – children, dogs, bags, bikes, boats. I saw a driver strap a dinghy to his bonnet. Off he went, round and round the bends, prow first, both hands on the horn this time. As a safety measure, he said.

The smart hotels are very smart. The oldest, La Palma, reclines in its own tropical garden and offers its guests secluded, shaded tables, from which they may watch the throng of expensive shoppers, glint-eyed over their Cartier and Vuitton.

These shops have always traded expensively. The Medicis used to come here for cameos in the fifteenth century. In the eighteenth century it was antiquities for the English. In the nineteenth century dandies, widows and homosexuals bought silver-backed brushes and gold cigarette cases, stacked beside souvenirs of Pompeii.

Now, day-trippers from Sorrento, on package-holiday outings, clog up the smooth flow of money and goods from trader to shopper. The beautiful ageless women and their slightly sinister iron-haired men have to compete at the luxury windows with red legs and bad haircuts, as the migrant shorts population wonders out loud how much everything costs before moving on to another ice cream.

At night, Capri partly reclaimed by the rich, the paparazzi hang about the entrance to the Quisisana, waiting to snap a film star or a scandal or, better still, both together.

A young hopeful stands in her evening wear in the doorway. She carries a silk handbag and her hair is dark as the sea. She's nobody. The cameras look the other way.

The Quisisana. The hotel where Oscar Wilde came after his release from prison. Signing himself as Sebastian Melmoth, he sat down wearily to eat his dinner, only to be asked by the manager to leave.

Those waiters in their white coats, those managers in their dark suits, the traders in linen dresses and hand-sewn shirts, know how much everyone is worth, and what something is worth to everyone. The balance between deference and manipulation is as timed to the second as the release brake on the funicular railway. Such tensions allow the system to run smoothly. The island itself is a tension between land and sea, height and depth. Poverty and riches have always lived on either side of the olive tree. The paradox of innocence and knowingness is in the faces of the young boys and the laughter of the girls. For Capri, the secret of success has been found in maintaining these tensions.

Not too slack, not too tight, that's Capri.

I was sitting at a bar in the square. Actually I was sitting in the square itself, so far had the bar extended its territory of bamboo chairs tucked beneath bamboo tables the size of saucers.

I had my laptop on my knee – there was nowhere else to put it – and I was drinking espresso with a slice of *torta Caprese*, when I saw you, just beyond the reach of the bar, crossing the square.

You were wearing a sleeveless dress and sandals, and I realised that you were one of those beautiful ageless women, and that the man with you, slightly sinister, has iron-grey hair. I know what I am – small, disappearing, an outsider – nobody would look at me twice even if they noticed me once. You were used to being looked at, I could see that.

You paused outside a shop selling heavy amethyst jewellery. The assistant appeared like a genie and soon had you bottled inside. That gave me the time I needed to pay my bill, pack my laptop and observe your husband. If it was your husband.

He had his hands in his pockets. Then he checked his watch. Then he put on his sunglasses. Then he went to look down over the harbour. Then he came back and paced outside the shop. Then he went and put a coin in the telescope. I guessed this was a man who went through life with a remote control, constantly flicking the channels. Finding nothing to interest him, he switched off and stared into space.

You came out of the shop and smiled like a movie star. You had a package. You took his arm. You talked all the time, pointing out this and that, and he nodded briefly, saw for a second, remembered consciously to enjoy himself.

I followed you both, not far, down to the Quisisana, and hid myself behind a gang of Americans and their tour leader. You were waiting at the lift, when suddenly you turned back and went towards the front desk. This was my chance – not to speak to you but to find out your room number. I got into the lift with your husband, got out with him on the third floor, and walked purposefully past him as he let himself into Room 29.

All right.

Now all I had to do was wait.

It was evening. The air like a kiss.

I was sitting on a low wall opposite the Quisisana. The paparazzi were joking with one another. A man with an accordion was playing on a balcony to a party of Japanese. I had been sitting for a couple of hours, carefully concealed behind my Dolce & Gabbana sunglasses, frames thin as the slit in a burka. I had not intended to be fashionable, merely I had bought my sunglasses in Italy, which amounts to the same thing.

I was typing on my laptop, trying to move this story on, trying to avoid endings, trying to collide the real and the imaginary worlds, trying to be sure which is which.

The more I write, the more I discover that the partition between real and invented is as thin as a wall in a cheap hotel room. I can hear voices on the other side, running water, the clink of bottles, the sound of a door opening and closing. When I get up and go out into the corridor, everything is silent, no one is there. Then, as soon as I reckon I know the geography of what isn't and what is, a chair scrapes in the room beyond the wall and a woman's voice says, 'You don't understand, do you?'

When I sit at my computer, I accept that the virtual worlds I find there parallel my own. I talk to people whose identity I cannot prove. I disappear into a web of co-ordinates that we say will change the world. What world? Which world?

It used to be that the real and the invented were parallel lines that never met. Then we discovered that space is curved, and in curved space parallel lines always meet.

The mind is a curved space. What we experience, what we invent, track by track running together, then running into one, the brake lever released. Atom and dream.

It was night.

He sauntered on to the terrace and was shown to a table by a waiter. Yes, I knew what she would be doing. I had seen it before.

I went quickly into the hotel, up to the third floor and along the corridor to Room 29. She was just coming out in a little black dress, scanning her face for the last time, before she snapped the silver mirror shut and slipped it back into her bag.

I stood still, waiting for her to finish.

She suddenly looked up, her face total surprise.

'What are you doing here?'
    'Aren't you pleased to see me?'
    'Yes. No, listen, I'm busy tonight.'
    'I saw.'
    'You've been spying on me.'
    'Only a little. Is he your husband?'
    She nodded.
    'How about tomorrow then – lunch?'
    She shook her head.
    'You choose a time then.'
    'How about the Middle Ages?'
    'The food isn't that good.'

She started walking down the corridor towards the lift. I kept up with her, though I didn't put out my hand. She was frowning and she didn't speak as we sped silently down in the moving hall of mirrors. When we got out into the lobby, she paused.

'This isn't a good idea.'
    'You told me you'd be here.'
    'I didn't think you'd come after me.'
    'Think of it as a coincidence.'
    'I have to go now. Walk out with me and say goodbye.'
    'Goodbye?'

'I don't want to get into explanations.'

'With me or with him?'

'With either of you.'

'So you'll just say I was someone you met in the lobby.'

'If he notices.'

'Depends what channel he's on.'

'What?'

'Never mind.'

'Don't make a scene, will you?'

'I'm not a playwright.'

'Ali?'

'Yes?'

'I'm sorry.'

She squeezed my hand and went over to her table. He stood up. There was a glass of champagne waiting.

'*Deux coupes de champagne*,' she had said in Paris. Now I suppose it was '*Due coppeta de champagne*.' Champagne, like English, is an international language. She spoke it fluently.

I hesitated, watching them, and then I decided to leave a note at the front desk. I wrote – 'Pizza Materita – Anacapri – until 10.30 p.m.'

I don't stay in Capri. It's too crowded, too expensive and too noisy for me. I rent a little place in Anacapri, high up on the hillside overlooking the sea. I read, swim, work and feed the stray cats on mince.

When I first came here, I realised from the pitying looks on the faces of the butchers that they thought of me as the Inglesa who only eats mince. This compounded the humiliation of asking every day for 'Half a pound of coffee-pot', as I seemed to have been doing. I had mixed up my *macchinetta* and my *macinato*. One is mince, the other is one of those steel coffee-pots they heat on the stove.

Anacapri is a small village high on the island. It has a busy square where the bus stops, and where the tourists go to get a chairlift up Monte Solano, followed by 'English Toast', as the sign encouragingly offers.

There are some smart shops leading off the square and the usual jostle of tourist stalls, but there is something else too, which I can't quite explain . . .

About halfway down the Via Orlandini, and for no reason at all that I can tell, an invisible fence rebuffs the tourists. They turn back. Yes, that is exactly what happens, they turn back.

If you continue, you will come to the true heart of Anacapri. There is the church. There is the square in front of it. There are greengrocers and a fishmonger and a bakery and market shops and a bookshop and a chemist and everything you could want. And no tourists.

So why am I not a tourist?

A tourist could be anywhere. The place doesn't matter. It's

just another TV channel.

I went to the bus stop in Capri and took my turn with the matrons and off-shift waiters to stand in the tiny, throaty diesel bullet of a bus that fires on all cylinders up the ladder-like road. The cliff face is netted to check falling rocks, and here and there a Madonna cut into the cliff face smiles down under her blue light.

I always cross myself as we reach a particular bend. So does the rest of the bus.

At the Piazza Monumentale out we get, and the women disappear with their string bags, and the men stand together for a moment, jackets slung over their shoulders, lighting cigarettes. I walk down towards the invisible fence and feel a slight tingle as I cross through it. Then I have been admitted. Then I am on the other side.

I know the people at the Pizza Materita, and they always find a table for me on their terrace, which overlooks the church and the square. I don't ask for anything straight away, but still somebody brings a jug of vino rosso and a breadbasket.

I can see Papa, with his long-handled paddle, ladling the pizzas in and out of the wood-fired oven. Nearby, Mama sits at the cash register, her glasses on a string round her neck. The daughter and the son-in-law deal with the customers. She is dark and gorgeous. He is young and good-looking, with his hair tied back like a pirate's.

The food is very good – all done to a secret recipe they say – and they are pleased with their cooking and each other and the new baby. You can taste the pleasure, strong as basil.

And then it happened as I thought it would. You came.

You had taken off the little black dress and you were wearing combat trousers and a hooded sweatshirt. That is, a hooded cashmere sweatshirt. Your hair was in a ponytail and the rings and the jewellery were gone.

You saw me, you came and sat down, your head in your hands for a second, then smiling.

'You bastard.'

'They only speak Italian here.'

'Very funny.'

'So why did you come?'

'Why do you think I came?'

'You are a Gemini and you have to be in two places at once.'

'Thanks for the cod astrology.'

'All right, here's some cod psychology – you had a row and stormed off.'

'I did, as it happens, that's how I'm free to be here, but not why.'

'OK. You tell me.'
'For this reason.'
She kissed me.

While we talked, our food was set before us. We both had bresaola with rocket and transparent slices of parmesan. Then for her there was a fresh fish wrapped in paper and baked in the wood oven. I had a pizza with a base as crisp as lava, bubbled here and there with a black crust and spread with buffalo mozzarella and tomatoes new off the vine.

I looked over into the square. Mothers and grandmothers were sitting chatting, while the men stood in groups. The children were playing some complicated version of hide and seek, using the church door as a touchline.

An Australian in shorts and boots, and a sweat-stained shirt, walked into the square and pulled a frisbee out of his backpack. He was slightly overweight, his girlfriend was tanned and rangy. They started surfing the frisbee to one another, carefully, quietly, she darting about, he standing still, always catching it as though he called it to him.

One by one the Italian children joined in, and then some of the parents, until the whole square was ringed with about twenty people playing frisbee. The Australians couldn't speak Italian and the Italians didn't bother to speak English. The rules, the form, the technique, were all conducted in sign language and body language, with laughter as the interpreter.

Imagine the square.

On one long side is the Pizza Materita. On the short side is the church. On the other long side is a smaller restaurant and a few houses. The fourth side of the square opens on to the street.

The church of Santa Sophia has a great door and niched on the right and left of the door, high up, are two symmetrical statues. One is San Antonio, the patron saint of Anacapri, and the other is the Madonna.

Imagine the square.

Excitement, laughter, the whizz-curve of the frisbee, new people pushing in, tired ones dropping out, then suddenly a boy throws the frisbee too high and too fast, and the purple plastic orb neatly hats the Madonna.

Allora! Mamma mia!

Nobody knows what to do.

Suddenly a matron in black comes forward. She takes the Australian by the hand and stands him below the statue. She crosses herself and gestures to him to do the same. Clumsily, he does it.

Then she shouts to her two sons – big heavy men in short-sleeved shirts. They too cross themselves before the Madonna and stand patiently on either side of the Australian.

The matron fetches her teenage grandchildren, stringy as beans. They cross themselves and are gestured upwards on to the shoulders of the three men, now arms round each other's waists, their feet braced apart.

The matron whistles, and a little kid, about three feet tall, comes running, and climbs, monkey-footed, up the human scaffolding. The base sweats. The teenagers complain, as hair, eyes, mouth and ears are tugged and pulled until the kid is upright. He leans forward to flip the frisbee off the Madonna. There is an imprecation from the ground. He looks down to see the matron shaking her fist at him. Guiltily he nods, crosses himself and tries again.

He has it at a grab and with a cry of pleasure turns round, his feet gripping into the shoulders of his cousins. Their hands clutch his thin ankles. He says something, they let him go and he jumps into space, both hands in the air, holding the frisbee like a parachute. He jumps into the air as if he were a thing of air, weightless, limitless, untroubled by gravity's insistence.

In the second's difference between flying and falling his mother has run forward. She catches him at a swing, taking both of them to the floor.

There she is, scolding and praising at the same time, while everybody gathers round, and wine is fetched from the restaurant, and ice cream in a bowl as big as a font.

Everybody salutes the Madonna. Madonna of the Plastic. Madonna of the Mistake. Madonna who sees all and forgives all. Madonna who can take a joke.

Tonight maybe, when the blinds are drawn and the square is

starlit and silent, the Madonna and San Antonio will laugh at the games, and talk over the events of the day, as they always do – watchers and guardians of the invisible life.

There are so many lives packed into one. The one life we think we know is only the window that is open on the screen. The big window full of detail, where the meaning is often lost among the facts. If we can close that window, on purpose or by chance, what we find behind is another view.

This window is emptier. The cross-references are cryptic. As we scroll down it, looking for something familiar, we seem to be scrolling into another self – one we recognise but cannot place. The co-ordinates are missing, or the co-ordinates pinpoint us outside the limits of our existence.

If we move further back, through a smaller window that is really a gateway, there is less and less to measure ourselves by. We are coming into a dark region. A single word might appear. An icon. This icon is a private Madonna, a guide, an understanding. Very often we remember it from our dreams. 'Yes,' we say. 'Yes, this is a world. I have been here.' It comes back to us like a scent from childhood.

These lives of ours that press in on us must be heard.

We are our own oral history. A living memoir of time.

Time is downloaded into our bodies. We contain it. Not only time past and time future, but time without end. We think of ourselves as close and finite, when we are multiple and infinite.

This life, the one we know, stands in the sun. It is our daytime and the stars and planets that surround it cannot be seen. The sense of other lives, still our own, is clearer to us in the darkness of night or in our dreams. Sometimes a total eclipse shows us in the day what we cannot usually see for ourselves. As our sun darkens, other brilliancies appear. And there is the strange illusion of looking over our shoulder and seeing the sun racing towards us at two thousand miles an hour.

What is it that follows me wherever I go?

She touched my hand and said, 'Will you always follow me?'

'Is life a straight line?'

'Isn't there a straight answer?'

'Not in my universe.'

'Which one is that?'

'The one curved by yours.'

'I love the curve of your back when you sleep,' she said.

'Then why did you get up and disappear that night in Paris?'

'I had to.'

'To save your skin?'

'To save my sense of self. You make me wonder who I am.'

'Who are you?'

'Someone who wants the best of both worlds.'

'So you do believe in more than one reality?'

'No. There's only one reality. The rest is a way of escape.'

'Is that what I am? An escape?'

'You said you wouldn't pin me to the facts.'

'The fact of your marriage?'

'Why do you keep thinking about it?'

'Because you do.'

She said something about life for her parents' generation. How it had been enough to raise a family, make a home, keep a job. Why isn't it enough any more? Why does everyone want to win the lottery or be a film star?

Or have an affair.

I took her hand. I was happy. I couldn't help it. She was here. I was happy.

'Come with me to the showjumping.'

'The what!'

'Concorso Ippico. Eleven o'clock tonight. Now.'

'You're mad.'

'No I'm not. I like horses. Come on.'

Looking at me very suspiciously, as intellectuals do when you mention animals, she took my hand and we walked together down the Via Boffe towards the Damacuta. Already we could hear the canned microphone voice of the commentator and see the floodlights of the stadium.

The air was hung with the scent of bougainvillaea, and as we walked past the muddle of houses crushed above the street, broken bars of music dropped through the open windows. A dog barked. Somebody turned up the television. There was the sound of a hosepipe and a trickle of water ran under our feet.

As we turned into the Damacuta, the route to the stadium was lit with flares. Kerosene had been poured into shallow terracotta saucers, each with a wick, and these flares, placed on the ground, lit up the feet of the crowds. We looked like gods with feet of fire. We looked like lovers blazing for each other.

Fire-paced, we found our way to the terraces and squatted right at the front with a load of children shouting excitedly about the horses. The loudspeakers were playing *Swan Lake*.

Then the riders came out, white jodhpurs, jackets off, to pace the distance between the jumps. This was to be a timed event; fastest time and fewest faults wins.

You said how great it would be if we all got a chance to walk the course before we had to compete.

I said we were walking the course all the time, but when the moment came to jump we still refused.

You glared at me.

Swan Lake was abruptly switched off. The judges assembled in the box, the commentator told us that the first rider was Swiss.

The bell rang. Out came horse and rider and, after a doff at the box, they were off, in a curved canter that sent the sand flying in flurries.

You were sitting right by the first jump, five feet high, and I heard your intake of astonishment at the effort of beauty and the beauty of effort, as the horse cleared the jump.

There's no such thing as effortless beauty – you should know that.

There's no effort which is not beautiful – lifting a heavy stone or loving you.

Loving you is like lifting a heavy stone. It would be easier not to do it and I'm not quite sure why I am doing it. It takes all my strength and all my determination, and I said I wouldn't love someone again like this. Is there any sense in loving someone you can only wake up to by chance?

Mister Archie, the Swiss horse, had a clear round, if a slow one. I was going to speak to you, but you were totally engrossed in the jumping.

The risks are interesting: do you aim for speed and a correspondingly greater risk of knocking off the poles, or do you take it steady and try for no faults?

The best riders manage both, but all riders are subject to the same rule: if a horse refuses to jump, he must be made to take it again. The rider must coax him round and convince him to do it. Horses have sudden fears.

So do I, but in this life you have to take your fences.

Later, walking home through the alleys as thin and black as the cats on every corner, you put your arm around me and asked again.

'Will you always follow me?'

'Who's following whom?'

'That's what I'm beginning to wonder.'

'There are two marks on a circle. Which is ahead? Which is behind?'

'Neither.'

'Then we're tailing each other.'

'Do you believe in fate?' she said, in that nervous way that people say it.

'Ye–es.'

'You don't sound so sure.'

'Fate isn't an excuse to let go of the reins.'

'OK, but what if you find you're riding a completely different horse?'

We were soon back at the place I had rented and I asked her if she was staying the night.

'So this time I don't have to beg?'

'I was the one who was the beggar tonight.'

She took me in her arms. 'I wish I could explain.'

'Explain what?'

'Oh, I know what you think of me.'

'What I think of you and what I feel for you are different things.'

'Do you usually sleep with people you despise?'

'That's not what I meant.'

'I want you to be my lover not my judge.'

She's right. I'm the one who's muddling things up. How she lives is her decision. If I don't like it I should stay out of the way. If I don't like it I should say so and close the door.

Her arms were warm and tight.

'What is it you want?' she said.

I want to be able to call you. I want to be able to knock on your door. I want to be able to keep your key and to give you mine. I want to be seen with you in public. I want there to be no gossip. I want to make supper with you. I want to go shopping with you. I want to know that nothing can come between us except each other.

We were lying together in the dark. The candle had burned out. Outside, the wind was whipping the canvas on the deckchairs. I could hear a plastic tumbler blowing round and round.

You were sleeping.

Why does nothing matter as much as this?

How do you seem to write me to myself?

I am a message. You change the meaning.

I am a map that you redraw.

Follow it. The buried treasure is really there. What exists and what might exist are windowed together at the core of reality. All the separations and divisions and blind alleys and impossibilities that seem so central to life are happening at its outer edges. If I could follow the map further and if I could refuse the false endings (the false starts don't matter), I could find the place where time stops. Where death stops. Where love is.

Beyond time, beyond death, love is. Time and death cannot wear it away.

I love you.

•

In the morning, thunder was rumbling round the island, the waves were white-topped and the birds were quiet.

I like islands because the weather is so changeable.

I like the way the morning can be stormy and the afternoon as clear and sparkling as a jewel in the water. Put your hand in the water to reach for a sea urchin or a seashell, and the thing desired never quite lies where you had lined it up to be. The same is true of love. In prospect or in contemplation, love is where it seems to be. Reach in to lift it out and your hand misses. The water is deeper than you had gauged. You reach further, your whole body straining, and then there is nothing for it but to slide in – deeper, much deeper than you had gauged – and still the thing eludes you.

I put the *macchinetta* on the stove and fed the cats the mince. At least I hope that's what I did. The little lizards were scuttling under the trailing vine and there was the usual earnest column of ants transporting a sliver of parmesan down to their hoard.

In the holm-oak, a blackbird had finished his morning bath in a pan of water I put out for him. In return he sings. He sings of the morning of the world, which happens every day for him, untainted by memory. The island is new. The tree has grown under his feet. His hollow bones are sung through with happiness. He flies light as a note.

The hiss and bubble of the coffee-pot reminded me of my business. I clattered out the little white cups on to the marble counter and poured the black, boiling coffee. Carefully I carried the two cups into the bedroom. The smell drifted into your dreams and you followed it back through sleep into day.

'What time is it?' you mumbled.

'Seven o'clock.'

'Horrible.'

You slumped back. I propped you up with pillows.

'You said you wanted to be woken early.'

'I didn't say the middle of the night.'

'It's been light for hours.'

'Not in my world it hasn't.'

'Drink this.'

You sipped noisily from the edge of the cup.

'Too strong.'

'I thought you like it strong.'

'A liquid should not be a solid.'

'It will get you going.'

'Going where?'

'Your hotel. Like you said.'

'Maybe I'll just stay here.'

'You can't.'

'Why not?'

'How many good reasons do you want?'

'Why don't you just go down there and get my clothes?'

'You want me to go and ask your husband for your clothes?'

'Yes.'

'I'm not Bugs Bunny.'

'What do you mean?'

'I mean that when he pulls off my head it won't flip back on again.'

'He won't pull your head off.'

'So what am I supposed to say?'

'Say I'm ill.'

'OK, you're ill, so you need all your little black dresses . . .'

'Of course I do.'

'Try again.'

'Say you're my cousin from Illinois.'

'I am not your cousin from Illinois.'

'For a writer you stick pretty close to the facts.'

'The fact is that your husband is down at the Quisisana.'

'The fact is that my lover is here ...'
She put down her coffee.
'In bed ...'
She leaned over and pulled me down on her.
'With me.'

It was ten o'clock before we got up again, which proves the pointlessness of early starts. I'm not a morning person, but some virtue still clings to it. People who stay up late (me) are debauched. People who get up early are clean living. Well, this morning, for once, I had got up early and look where it had led me.

A second pot of coffee was bubbling on the stove. You must have caught a whiff of conscience because you suddenly said –
'I ought to call him.'
'There's no phone here.'
'Where's your mobile?'
'In London.'
'What's it doing there?'
'Absolutely nothing.'
'So where can I find a phone?'
'I don't know. In the square maybe.'
'I'll walk up.'
'I'll come with you.'
'Look, maybe I should go.'

'That's not what you said three hours ago.'

'Don't bully me.'

'I'm not bullying you.'

'It isn't my fault that you don't have a phone.'

'It isn't my fault that you're married.'

'Not this again.'

'What – does it weary you, my love?'

'Yes, it does, as it happens.'

'Well, just fuck off.'

'What?'

'I said fuck off.'

'Fine. That's fine.'

She was out of the place, taking the steep steps two at a time and disappearing up the vertical alleys before I could fumble with the Calor gas of the stove, grab the keys and go after her.

'You should let her go,' I'm saying to myself, my legs taking no notice. 'For God's sake, let her go,' and my heart was pounding and I was angry, so angry, with myself or her, I don't know. Just blood pushing against thought. Angry at me or her, and my fist clenched round the keys as I bounded up the track, hearing the church bell like a pulse.

When I got to the Piazza Monumentale, I saw her disappearing in one of the white taxis with the roof down. I ran over to the rank. Stopped. I had come out without any money. Ripping through my pockets all I could produce was a five-thousand-lire note.

OK. The bus.

I stood in the queue, the sun too hot, no sunscreen, sweating like a horse, my mouth dry, my face like a gargoyle (no sunglasses), my blood pressure at hospital level and my heart melting like a tourist's ice cream.

For half an hour, bus after bus came in the opposite direction, and I kept saying to myself, 'Get on, go down to the Faro, swim as you are, wash her off you.' But it was too late for that, so I stood there like an idiot, waiting.

The bus finally arrived and I shoved on and darted for an orange plastic seat. This was hardly the stuff of romance. If I had been writing about it, I could have come out with more money. I would have remembered my sunglasses, ordered a soundtrack. As it was, the bus skidded and honked down to the terminus, and a woman with one fat hand on the chrome rail and another fat hand round a bag of onions kept digging her heel into my foot. When I got off I was limping.

So this is me – sweating like a horse, looking like a dog, limping like a chicken, poor as a church mouse and jumpy as a flea – heading for the Quisisana, where, naturally enough, the doorman won't let me in. And you know what? I can't even bribe him.

After a lot of bad Italian, I did manage to persuade him to call Room 29.

Any answer?

Niente.

I slunk off, past the Cartier and Vuitton, past the bar where I couldn't afford a drink, past the sneering waiters and the gold bracelet man at the Cambio, whose single split-second glance said, 'Pauper.'

I crept back to the oily floor of the bus terminus and bought my ticket back to Anacapri. I was so thirsty that I could have unscrewed the radiator cap of the bus and dropped a straw in it – if I had a straw, or if I could have bought one. I made up my mind never to put myself in a situation like this again. As we changed up from the ear-splitting second gear into life-threatening third, I prayed to the Madonna of the Falling Rocks to give me the good sense not to crush myself.

night screen

Night. Screen. Tap tap tap. Tap tap. Tap.

The coded message that anyone can read.

I keep telling this story – different people, different places, different times – but always you, always me, always this story, because a story is a tightrope between two worlds.

VIEW AS ICON

There is no greater grief than to find no happiness but happiness in what is past.

This is the story of Francesca da Rimini and her lover Paolo. You can find it in Boccaccio. You can find it in Dante. You can find it here.

My father's castle is built of stone. The stone is thick as darkness. Darkness is to the inside what stone is to the outside of this castle; impenetrable, unscalable, a stone-dark heavy as thought.

The dark stone weighs on us. Our thoughts bear us down. We roll the dark in front of us down the icy corridors, and in the rooms the darkness accumulates, sits in our chairs, waits. We wait.

The castle is a pause between dark and dark. It fills the space between a man's thoughts and his deeds. My father made the design for the castle himself. It is as though we are living inside him.

Inside the castle, the furniture is black oak from Spain. In the one room where we keep a fire there is a long black table with candlesticks. At this table, for the first time, I saw Paolo.

Paolo il bello . . .

My father Guido had long been at war with Malatesta, Lord of Rimini. A marriage was planned as a condition of peace, and Paolo rode in retinue to wild Ravenna to fetch me.

We lit the dark hall with candles, which forced the darkness off a little, made it crouch in strange shapes, like a thing whipped.

We dressed ourselves in black, my mother and I, for my father told us that every day is a day of mourning. I wore no adornment, but my hair is as loose and flowing as the cataract that roars under my window, and just as the cataract is tamed to the waterwheel, my hair is tamed to the braid, but both escape.

I bound myself as tightly as I could and went downstairs.

There was a curious light in the room. It was not the fire nor the candles nor the effect of the storm outside. I did not dare raise my eyes to discover the source, but walked mute and downcast towards the table, where my father presented me to Paolo.

I did not look up. I offered him my hand and he kissed it and placed a ring on my finger.

Through our meal my father talked only to the envoys and said nothing to Paolo or myself. I heard Paolo's voice talking to my mother, and the music of it was like a flute or a pipe. I wanted to see him, but I had not the power.

At the end of our meal my mother and father and all the envoys and servants left the room abruptly. None of the dishes had been cleared and the wine was left spilt on the table. I could sense Paolo looking at me.

There was a low rumbling noise, like a scaffold being wheeled out, and from the shadow on the floor, I understood that a great canopied bed had been pushed into the room.

I did not raise my eyes, but my skin was as cold as wax.

I heard Paolo get up and, coming round to my side of the table, he took my hand and bade me stand up.

'Francesca,' he said, 'let me see your breasts.'

I could not move, but his hands were sure as falcons and he soon had me pinned under him.

We lay on the bed and he kissed me – nothing more – one hand on my breast, the other gently stroking himself, until he felt my kisses meet his, and then he took my hand to where his own was active, and now freed, began to open my legs.

The pleasure was as shocking as the thought of pleasure.

The next morning, both dressed in white, we passed through the walls of my father's castle as easily as ghosts. In my whole life I had never been beyond the shadow of the castle. The shadow-tip of the flag marked the limit of my walks and my own shadow followed me wherever I went.

Today was not like that.

Today was sun and sky and birdsong and open faces, and I blessed my father's war, which had made this love.

As we rode, the light went with us. He was the light.

Paolo il bello.

My lover, my loved one, my love.

I need not tell how we passed our days as we rode in splendour along the coast. There was such lightness in me that I had to be tied to the pommel of the saddle to keep myself from bird height. I was bold as a starling. You fed me from your own plate. My eyes were always watching you. I thought you were one of the angels from the church window. We flew together, your wings in gold leaf from the sun. Time flew with us, and very soon we were in sight of your father's lands.

I noticed a change in you — a dampening and a quiet that I did not understand. I thought you were ashamed of me, but you shook your head, your beautiful head like an angel, and asked me to wait.

I did wait. I had waited before now. Waited all my life, it seemed. 'What is life', my father had said, 'but a waiting for death?'

Then there were trumpets and running feet and crowds gathering and pennants and a team of white horses in silver harnesses and the white horses drew a carriage and in the carriage was a strange swarthy misshapen man, dressed all in leather, his fingers full of rings.

You turned to me and your voice was breaking as water breaks against a rock it cannot wear away.

'That man is to be your husband,' you said. 'That man, my brother.'

Oh Paolo, *il bello*, why did you lie to me?

Say you are lying to me now.

The wedding took place that afternoon.

My husband was scarcely four feet tall and as twisted in body as Paolo was straight. These things need not have been laid to his fault, but his heart was his own making and his heart was as unformed by kindness as his body had been neglected by beauty. He cared for nothing but hunting and women, and he lashed his dogs and his whores with the same strap.

The horrors of my nights with him might have been bearable if I had not been taught a different way. The grave of my childhood life and the grave of my married life might have crumbled into one another without distinction, if Paolo had not kissed me and raised me from the dead for those few wide-open days.

Then, months later, when my husband was away, Paolo came into my room. He suggested we might read together to while away the time, and this was approved with a short nod from my waiting woman who was paid to be my gaoler.

Every morning Paolo came to me, and we read together the

story of Lancelot du Lac, and his love for Queen Guinevere.

We read out loud, and there were many pauses, many broken sighs and swift glances, and as we bent our heads lower and lower over the page, to scribe a private world, our cheeks met, and then our lips, and he was honey in my mouth as I kissed him.

There was no more time for reading that day.

We contrived it – oh, I don't know how – to be together, alone with our book, though we never turned another page.

Paolo, your love for me was a clear single happiness, and I would not give it up to save my soul.

He caught us. You know he did. Perhaps he trapped us. He might have done.

We were in bed together, naked, hot, Paolo inside me, when Gianciotto burst through the door with his men. I saw his face, triumphant, malign, and I saw him raise his terrible hand. He had a hand made of iron that he had fashioned into a spike. It was this hand that he ran through Paolo's smooth back, and through into my belly and my spine, and into the flock of the mattress. The force was so great that it lifted him up and pinned him above us like a weathercock.

I put my hands to Paolo's bleeding body, and he said to me, so that only I could hear –

'There is no love that does not pierce the hands and feet.'

He was dead then, and I dead under him, and hand in hand our souls flew down the corridors and out of his brother's palace as easily as our bodies had done when we left my father's house.

I have never let go of his hand.

We are as light now as our happiness was, lighter than birds. The wind carries us where it will, but our love is secure.

No one can separate us now. Not even God.

blame my parents

Night. The window is open. Thousands of miles away your tears tap tap on the board. If your make-up is run-proof, my heart isn't.

'Is this how it ends?' you said.
　　'It isn't ended yet.'
　　'If only you could accept me as I am.'
　　'This is where the wheel spins and spins.'
　　'We just dig ourselves in deeper.'
　　'We know all the common-sense solutions.'
　　'You make it sound like floor cleaner.'
　　'I don't know how to give you up,' I said.
　　'You could rewrite the story.'
　　'I've tried. Haven't you noticed?'
　　'Isn't there a better ending than either/or?'
　　'I can't write it.'
　　'Bloody bloody absolutist.'
　　'Blame my parents.'

'For the wild look in your eyes?'

'For telling me that the treasure is really there.'

'I don't understand.'

'Some things are worth looking for all your life.'

'You weren't looking for me.'

'No, and I wasn't looking for love either.'

'Then what happened?'

Then. Then what? Then what happened? What can I say? I like being on my own better than I like anything else, but I can't give up love. Maybe it's the tension between longing and aloneness that I need. My own funicular railway, holding in balance the two things most likely to destroy me.

I said, 'Perhaps there are a few things you should know.'

'About you?'

'About what makes me what I am.'

'You can't blame your parents for everything.'

'I don't blame them for anything.'

'So?'

'So do you want to hear this story?'

'Tell it.'

EMPTY TRASH

I was adopted by a man and a woman who owned a Muck
Midden. They had no children of their own and they wanted me
to be their little muck-mole – to shuffle and snuffle through the
daily cast-off of the all-consuming world.

They were superstitious people. The kind of people who
kept a rabbit's paw in each pocket and a crucifix round the neck,
just in case.

They knew, with some squint-eyed sweaty knowledge that
had never been learned, that by themselves they could never find
anything in muck but muck. They were muck-solid, muck-sure.
They had no trouble with muck.

And yet . . .

And yet an orphan was what they wanted. A changeling
child. A child without past or future. A child outside of time who
could cheat time. A lucky bag. A charm. The smallest silver key
on the heavy keyring. The key that opens the forbidden door.

To get an orphan they had to visit the orphanage.

They put on their best clothes. They squeezed their feet into hostile shoes. They caught the bus to the orphanage and the warden showed them inside.

'Pink room or Blue?'

(Choice. Panic. They whispered to one another hastily.)

The warden tapped her foot on the linoleum.

(Girls are cheaper, easier, cleaner.)

'Pink, please.'

Back home, at the Muck House, Mrs M buttered the loaf for corned-beef sandwiches with pickled onions, while Mr M threw another car tyre on the fire. They were warm and fed. They loved their baby.

'How much do you love her?' asked Mr M.

'As much as a pram with its wheels off,' said Mrs M. 'How much do *you* love her?'

'More than two bags full of washing-machine hoses,' said Mr M.

The baby gurgled and played with its little necklace of spent bullets strung across the cot.

'Is this where the treasure starts?' said Mr M.

'Read the signs,' said his wife.

But he couldn't read the signs because he couldn't read.

My parents called me Alix because they wanted a name with an X in it, because X marks the spot.

I was the one who would find the buried treasure.

That there was treasure they never doubted. My father dug so fiercely at the end of the rainbow that part of the kitchen subsided.

They were always out – on full moons, on new moons, with a box of magic mongoose droppings and a metal detector.

Metals were my domain.

I learned how to strip a fridge of its cooling unit, thermostat and plug. I unwound miles of copper wire from millions of solenoids. I separated zinc from lead, lead from iron, iron from steel, steel from tin.

My father made me a bed from a galvanised water trough. My mother lined it with flock from an old mattress.

One night, when she was tucking me up under the eiderdown, my feet on an old car radiator that served as a hot-water bottle, I asked her what the red stamp on the side of my bed meant.

'That's a word,' she said.

'What word is it?'

'CATTLE.'

'What's a cattle?'

'More cows than one.'

She went out and I traced the word with my finger – CATTLE.

Reading and writing were both forbidden at the Muck House.

My mother could do both, my father could do neither, therefore they had no value.

What had value were starter motors, carburettors, twelve-volt batteries, three-core cable, push buttons, switches and car seats battered as prizefighters.

In the workshop in the scrapyard my father assembled unbadged monster cars; petrol-driven Frankensteins, bolted together on oversize wheels.

I was his pit-monkey. I was the one who crouched under the chassis in the oil-stained well. I handed him his hammers and swivel joints, and freed the seized metalwork by swinging off a ratchet bar with all my weight. Suddenly the thing would give, and I would drop down, scraping hands and knees on the dirty concrete. Then, stumbling for my spanners, I would climb the steps and begin again.

It was night. The stars were out, metallic and contained. My mother was putting me to bed.

'Write me a word,' I said.

'There's no reading or writing here.'

'Write me a word that goes with CATTLE. No one will notice.'

Of course there was no one to notice, except my father.

Carefully, and with many glances at the door, my mother wrote in red letters on my galvanised trough-bed – TUBERCULOSIS.

'Is that a cattle word?'

'Yes.'

'What word would you give me if you could?'

'I can't. There's no use for words here.'

'But if you could?'

She scribbled on a piece of cardboard out of her pocket, and pressed it into my hand, nervously, afraid.

'Never show this to anyone.'

GENTLENESS.

My father had a supply of large glass jars with lead seals. He stored in these hydrogen peroxide, mercury, prussic acid, solutions of nitrate, ammonia. Hazardous liquids were not my domain and I was forbidden to go into the cellar.

One day, when my father was out collecting scrap, I took a flashlight and crept down the thirteen steps into the cellar. I told myself I wanted an apple. We kept them wrapped in newspaper through the winter. There they were, each by each on slatted racks, smelling the cellar of fruit and autumn.

I took my apple, folding the paper carefully because in scrap nothing can be wasted. We *were* waste.

Then I turned my flashlight on to the jars – the deep blue and pale green of the jars. Some were cloudy, one was red. I had no idea what any of them could be, for although I was secretly learning to read, my father wrote his labels as a chemist would – FE, H_2O, H_2N, NH_2, AS_2, O_3.

I went closer, standing on tiptoe, muttering the symbols to myself.

At the end of a row of jars coloured like dreams was an opaque jar with a heart drawn on it and a dagger through the heart. I put up my hand to touch it, and in that second my hand was grabbed from behind.

It was my father. He put his face close to mine, and I could smell the sulphur on him.

'Never touch that jar. Never. If that ever gets loose we're finished.'

'What is it?'

'Love,' said my father. 'There's love in that jar.'

And so I discovered that love is a hazardous liquid.

One day I asked my mother –

'Is there a world beyond here?'

She shook her head and stretched out her arms end to end.

'Nothing but waste and scrap. The earth itself is nothing but a collection of belched rocks and burning gases. We live in a cosmic dustbin.'

'Is the lid on or off?'

'On. Nobody gets beyond the dustbin.'

'Well, where's the buried treasure then?'

Her eyes lit up like a couple of sodium street lamps. 'That's for *you* to find.'

At night, my father blazed up the fire with a can of petrol and my mother told stories from her youth. Her youth was like a far-off city where she had lived for a time and been happy. She had all the longing of an exile for a place where she could never return.

Like other exiles, her longing grew a narrative of its own. Her desire told itself as memory. Her past was a place that none of us could visit without her. It was the only kingdom she could control.

'I used to live on a river,' she said. 'A river stocked so full with fish so fat that anyone who wanted to cross to the other bank just walked over the fishes' backs as though they were stones.

'In those days no one went fishing. No one had ever heard of fishing. If a housewife wanted a few brown trout for supper, she would take her skillet down to the river, and shout, "YOU, YOU AND YOU," and the fish would jump into the pan, tame as fleas.'

'Are fleas tame?' I said.

'They were in those days,' she said, and continued . . .

'In those days, everyone carried a little handbell in their pockets, and if you wanted to speak to someone, you stood outside their door and rang your bell. The person inside would say, "Is that my bell I hear ringing?" and you would reply, "No, it's not your bell, it's mine." Then they would say, "Well, if it's not my bell, I won't answer it," and you would know you were not wanted, but if they said, "Well, well, since it's your bell, I'll answer it for you," you would know you would be welcome.'

'Where's your bell?' I said.

'You'll get it when I die,' she said, and continued ...

'In those days, anyone hunting in the woods found buried treasure – only it wasn't really buried – it was lying on the surface and there was such a lot of it.

'I remember once walking out hand in hand with a boy I knew, and it was summer, and suddenly before us was a field of gold. Gold as far as you could see. We knew we'd be rich for ever. We filled our pockets and our hair. We were rolled in gold. We ran through the field laughing and our legs and feet were coated in yellow dust, so that we were like golden statues or golden gods. He kissed my feet, the boy I was with, and when he smiled, he had a gold tooth.

'It was only a field of buttercups, but we were young.'

'Will I ever be young?' I asked my mother.

It was bedtime and my father was winding the clock.

'You are young,' said my father. 'You won't get any younger even if you clean your teeth twice a day.'

'You'll get older,' said my mother, 'that's what happens.'

'Then what happens?'

'You won't be able to find the treasure.'

'Will I be too old to look for it?'

'No, but you'll be looking in the wrong place.'

'Why doesn't everyone find the treasure?'

'Some people say there's no such thing.'

'That's because they've never found it.'

'And other people don't know where to look.'

My mother and father both wore spectacles. I took my mother's off her nose and tried to see through them. The world was blurred and strange.

'I can't see anything through these. Can you?'

My mother looked away, my father looked into the clock. There was a little beetle under the coalscuttle. There were three ebony elephants with ivory tusks on the mantelpiece. There was a brass cone for holding tapers. The bevelled mirror on its chain had come out of a better house than ours; its scrollwork was angels and streamers. By the fire was a tin bucket overflowing with old money and foreign coins – the kind of loot that fell out of dismantled seat webbing, or was tipped up from the backs of house-clearance drawers. None of it was worth anything, but we collected it anyway, and when my parents were brooding, one or the other would scoop up a handful of coins and throw them on to the fire, shouting, 'Money to burn!'

I watched it burn. I watched the monarch's heads bleed out their alloy, the cheap pre-war French francs bend and twist like silver foil. The best coins were the true copper pennies that burned from orange to blue – an Aladdin's lamp blue, or the underside of dragon's wings, or the green you get from goblins.

I loved the fire. The coals were my books. Heated to story temperature, they burst into flame and I read in them the stories that no one would read to me.

'What can you see?'

It was my mother's voice roaring from miles away. I shook out of my trance by the fire.

'Another world.'

'There isn't one.'

I pointed to the road winding through the flames. She was angry with me.

'The fire will be out soon enough. There's nothing in the ashes but ash.'

She went to bed. My father went to bed too. They left me alone as they usually did, to sleep and half-wake by the dying fire. When the novelty of myself had worn off, they had given up tucking me into my galvanised bed and I either went there or not, as I felt.

The fire was grey. The road was gone. I had to stay young. I had to look in the right place. I had to keep the fire going. I had to believe in the treasure. I had to find the treasure too.

SPECIAL

In 1999 mountaineers on Everest found a body.

There was nothing unusual about that – Everest is grave to many. What was unusual is that the body had been missing since 1924 and had lain preserved and unnoticed, keeping its blank vigil for seventy-five years.

The body was George Mallory.

On the morning of 6 June 1924 Mallory and his climbing partner, Andrew Irvine, made a breakfast of sardines, took their oxygen cylinders and began to climb Everest one last time.

It was Mallory's third expedition. Always the men were beaten back. No matter how high they climbed, Everest was higher.

By now, the rest of their party were unfit, frost-bitten, snow-blind and altitude sick. Irvine's skin was peeling off his face due to freezing air temperatures contrasted with 120°F in the sun. The camp was ready to break up. Mallory argued for a final attempt. His colleagues thought he was in poor condition and mentally unstable.

After two days and nights climbing the mountain, Mallory, Irvine and the team of sherpas had moved up from the North Col to Camp VI. It had been Mallory's brainwave, as he called it, to set up a series of camps on the ascent route. Camp VI was just a two-man tent perched on a ridge. The climbers arrived. The sherpas set off back to the North Col. Tomorrow was everything. Tomorrow was nothing. Curled up, breathing oxygen, the men slept.

Day came. Mallory climbed. He had never climbed so well. His fingers and feet made a way across the ridges and rotten limestone so that he seemed to be an evolving part of the mountain itself. The mountain is endlessly moving, shifting, changing itself. Mallory was moving with it, using its un-detectable flow as a rhythm for his own body. He sang the mountain, and the mountain, sharp, high, outside of human range, heard and sang back.

Irvine followed. Young, inexperienced, faithful, he would have followed Mallory anywhere. His fingers and toes went trustingly into the openings that Mallory noted. Every note took them higher up the octave of the mountain. They scaled impossible flats, vertical sharps. Mallory's body was natural to the mountain.

The two men were last sighted at 12.50 p.m. on 8 June 1924.

One of the team, Odell, had climbed behind them, up to

Camp VI, and as he scanned the summit for a sign, he suddenly saw first one dark shape, then a second, moving rapidly towards the final peak. Then the clouds hid them from view.

It began to snow. Mallory hardly noticed. He was light, clean, with a crystal music in his head of the kind he had heard the Tibetan monks play in the monastery at Rongbuk. There was nothing to fear. There was only the forward movement of the ascent, and his heart beating time.

Why could he hear his heart? The thought came and went.

He was thirsty. They had lost their stove and hadn't been able to thaw any ice. The oxygen had run out. He was very cold, but his fingers and toes went without fault into the bands of the rock. Irvine was struggling now, but there was nothing to worry about. Mallory would pull him up on a rope. He would pull him up now because they were there.

The top of Everest, which is the top of the world, is about the size of a billiard table. Mallory had played the game and won. Only it didn't feel like a game, it felt like music. The mountain was one vast living vibration. Again he heard the piercing sounds in his head, and underneath them his pulse.

He pulled Irvine towards him on the thin rope. He banged his watch and the glass broke. He started to laugh and then he couldn't stop laughing, because it was so silly really, his watch going tick, tick, tick, when time had stopped long since and there was no time. Not here. They were outside time, he knew that.

They were quiet, the two men, and the mountain was quiet too. She wasn't used to visitors. Not here.

Irvine was shaking uncontrollably, though Mallory was still. As seeming-still as the mountain he was becoming.

They began their descent.

Irvine's body has never been found, though some claim it has been sighted.

Mallory was lying face down, his back and shoulders naked and white and changed into a part of the mountain. He was identified from the label in his clothes –

W.F. Paine. High St. Godalming. G. Mallory.

He had climbed Everest in his old tweed jacket.

In his inside pocket, frozen against his heart, was his last letter from his wife.

Unfold it. Read it. She loves him. She wants him to come home. His children miss him. The garden is lovely.

Her eyes are dark. His are pale.

Mallory fell. We don't know how. He was found in the self-arrest position with a broken body and closed eyes. His broken watch was in his pocket. There was no more time.

own hero

In this life you have to be your own hero.

By that I mean you have to win whatever it is that matters to you by your own strength and in your own way.

Like it or not, you are alone in the forest, just like all those fairy tales that begin with a hero who's usually stupid but somehow brave, or who might be clever, but weak as straw, and away he goes (don't worry about the gender), cheered on by nobody, via the castles and the bears, and the old witch and the enchanted stream, and by and by (we hope) he'll find the treasure.

On the day I was born I became the visible corner of a folded map.

I was not born to wealth. I was born to mind the machine. My parents and grandparents were weavers. They worked in the shuttering sheds that broke the line of the valley with their tall chimneys. They worked twelve-hour days and went deaf in their forties. They bred their own kind, as sheep and pigs do, but human kind is not sheep and pigs. They bred me, unexpected, unwanted. They bred me, and whether it was desperation, or a sixth sense for trouble, they gave me away. They didn't give away any of the others, before or after, but me they did, and quickly too.

They gave me away to my fate without even a card in the Post Office window, saying 'Good Home Wanted'. Good home, bad home, no home, it was all the same to them, and they left no bundle beside me for the journey.

Life was a journey I would have to make by myself.

Myself. If they gave me nothing, that was the one thing they could not take away.

I think of myself sometimes, unable to walk, unable to crawl, lying in my cot and listening to the sound of the trams on their metal rails. At night, outside the window, there was a room opposite with a big globe pendant light made of white china. It looked like the moon. It looked like another world.

I used to watch it until the image of it became sleep, and until the last tram whooshed past, the bend in the road made audible by the air concertina'd in the rubber pleats that joined the cars.

The globe and the tram were my companions and the certainty of them, their unfailingness, made bearable the smell of sour milk and the high bars of the cot and the sound of feet on the polished oilcloth – feet always walking away.

My mother, they say, was a little red thing out of the Manchester mills, who at seventeen gave birth to me, easy as a cat.

Her voice was soft – like the river over the chalk pan of the riverbed. You will say I never heard it, but I heard it every day in the nine months that I was her captive or she was mine.

I knew her voice and I must have seen her face once, mustn't I?

Voice and face are homed somewhere in me as I was homed in her. It was a brief eternity waiting for time to begin. Then time tumbled me out, cut me loose, and set the clock – RUN! RUN! Put as much distance as you can between you and then.

To avoid discovery I stay on the run. To discover things for myself I stay on the run.

meatspace

Night. I'm sitting at my screen, wondering how this story might develop. An envelope flies in front of my face. I open it. What else can you do?

'Ali. I'm coming to London.'
    (I'd better reply. What else can you do?)
    'Business or pleasure?'
    'I want to see you.'
    'I thought we weren't seeing each other.'
    'We're not.'
    'Are you going to keep your eyes closed then?'
    'I'd always know you in the dark.'
    'Cut it out.'
    'Where do you live?'
    'You've got my Website.'
    'Meatspace not cyberspace.'
    'Spitalfields.'
    'Where?'

'I live in Spitalfields.'

'Sounds revolting.'

'It's right in the City. Roman London, Falstaff London, Dickens London.'

'What's the name and number?'

'VERDE'S. Ask for the old market.'

'Verde? Like Italian? Like green?'

'You'll see it. It's an old house . . .'

spitalfields

This part of the city is an emperor's maze of streets that darken into alleys, and alleys that blank into walls. The noise of the river is nearby, but the water itself is unseen. It is as though the water is everywhere and nowhere, perhaps under the streets, perhaps inside the houses, with their watery windows where the old glass reflects the light.

This part of the city has always been a place for refugees. Exile or sanctuary, they come here and have done since the Huguenots with their bales of cloth, since the Bengalis with their sweatshops, and since the quiet people from Hong Kong with their money.

Beside all of this has always been the life of the traders – English, Spanish, Dutch, selling gassed oranges and arsenals of lemons the size of hand grenades.

The yellow faces of the Chinamen were once downriver where the opium boats came in. Now the yen trades with the euro and alongside the oldest profession, which has always thrived here and still does – the short skirts by the hot-dog stand in front of the church.

In an old part of the city like this, time collapses the picture.

Here I am, tightrope walking the twenty-first century, slim as a year, and the old tall houses are two hundred years old and set on streets that wind back four hundred years, set on cart tracks that served medieval monks. Or Shakespeare. Or Dr Johnson and his friend Boswell the Scot. They all walked here. Put any of them here now and they would still recognise the place.

Put me here now and that single year's rope, stretched towards the future, is all I have to balance me from the drop on either side.

There's an Indian grocer's here. Bundles of coriander make a hedge between shop and pavement, and behind are the trays of chillies and stacked-up cartons of long-life milk.

Every week the frozen fish van arrives, and two Bengalis drag out something the size of Moby Dick. Two more stagger out to the pavement with a steel workbench and a circular saw. Moby Dick is slabbed on to the steel. The saw screams. The unnameable grey-coloured fish is neatly bagged into curry-sized portions.

Next door, the Halal butcher gently drains the blood of a sheep into a plastic bath.

'When I first came here as a boy,' an old cab driver tells me, 'the first morning I woke up, I looked out of the window and there was a street market going on in Petticoat Lane and a bloke selling a lion cub – sitting like a cat it was, washing its paws – just like a cat of yours or mine.

'Over there was a strong man in chains, freeing hisself, and then a Black Shirt got up, you know, one of Mosley's Fascists, and he made a speech and then a fight broke out, and there was a whistle, and the police came running down from Brick Lane, only nobody got caught because the gutter was thick with offal from the meat stall, and half of the coppers slipped on it and the other half fell over them.'

Ask anyone round here for a story and you'll get one.

The archaeologists were digging here yesterday. They uncovered a stone sarcophagus shielding a decorated lead coffin.

It had been there for one thousand eight hundred years.

The guess is that inside the coffin will be the Roman Governor of London, his body basted in a plaster and chalk mix used as a disinfectant.

They dug him up when they were excavating the foundations of a new bank – the kind of Temple to Mammon that the Governor would have approved of. Maybe that's why they chose the site. Maybe he was what attracted them, although they could never admit it. Maybe through all the talk of land value and client access and transport links and investment opportunity, maybe behind the glassy eyes of the Chief Accountant, maybe in the dreams of the Chairman of the Board, maybe floating under the skin of a thousand cups of coffee at a hundred planning meetings, maybe between the lines of the shiny facts and figures sent out to the shareholders, maybe in the tremble of the blood inside the hand that held the pen that signed the cheque that bought the site, was the will of a dead man waiting for his final tribute.

Far-fetched?

The past is magnetic. It draws us in. We cannot help ourselves and, as with other things that we cannot help in ourselves, we make up elaborate explanations, reasonable rational explanations, to chant away the powerful things that don't belong to us.

There he is, coming slowly up the Thames in his rowed barge. That's him, the one with the cropped hair and the clean fingernails.

On either side of the broad river are marshes and dull sand, and deeper in are forests as tight-grown as a cash crop. But these forests are wild and the unseen eyes that watch him are as far from civilisation as he is from home.

His men have lit a brazier in the prow of the boat. They use it to keep warm. They use it as a light. The olive stones they use as fuel burn down to a powder, and when a man rakes it he smells his homesickness in the sharp salty greenness of the fire.

So the boat slips on, and to the eyes watching in the forest it is the fire itself coming upriver. The fire moving steadily through the dark and the mist. The impossibility of fire and water. The fire that will spread into the trees, into the settlements, into the huts of the Britons themselves, until all resistance has been burned away.

Or has it?

The forests can be levelled and the roads made straight, but the wild things go deeper, beyond detection, and wait.

'*Open it . . .*'
   'Everybody ready?'
   '*For Christ's sake, open it!*'

The sarcophagus is surrounded by men in green masks, as though this site were an operating theatre. Outside the TV crews and the journalists are waiting for the most significant discovery yet unearthed in Roman London.

'When we see his body, it will tell us everything.'
   'The kind of man he was, his power . . .'
   'OK. Everybody ready? Here we go.'

With infinite care, the side of the tomb is being opened. A trickle of brown water seeps out.

'*Oh Christ. How did that get in there?*'
'This thing should be airtight, waterproof.'
'It was bombproof. It has survived eighteen hundred years.'
'*Bombproof but not waterproof, huh?*'
'Shut up and open it.'

Cloth of gold, leaves, mud, a skeleton. Serious water damage . . .
And . . .

'Look at the pelvis.'
'What?'
'It's a woman.'

HELP

You had come to London.

We were in bed together, watching the sun stream through the window. I was happy in a sad sort of way, because I knew this was never going to work.

Work. Not work. What do I mean?

If someone had told Mallory that he would climb Everest but die in the attempt, still he would have climbed it.

What does the end matter?

Here, now, is enough, isn't it?

You had once asked me if I was afraid of death.

I said I was afraid of not living.

I don't want to eke out my life like a resource in short supply. The only selfish life is a timid one. To hold back, to withdraw, to keep the best in reserve, both overvalues the self, and undervalues what the self is.

Here's my life – I have to mine it, farm it, trade it, tenant it, and when the lease is up it cannot be renewed.

This is my chance. Take it.

You rolled over so that I could stroke your back.

Sex between women is mirror geography. The subtlety of its secret – utterly the same, utterly different. You are a looking-glass world. You are the hidden place that opens to me on the other side of the glass. I touch your smooth surface and then my fingers sink through to the other side. You are what the mirror reflects and invents. I see myself, I see you, two, one, none. I don't know. Maybe I don't need to know. Kiss me.

You kiss me and the glass grows cloudy. I stop thinking. Meatspace still has some advantages for a carbon-based girl.

Dear love – with your hair like a bonfire that somebody kicked over – red, spread out, sparks flying. I don't want to conquer you; I just want to climb you. I want to climb through the fire until I am the fire.

Love has got complicated, tied up with promises, bruised with plans, dogged with an ending that nobody wants – when all love is, is what it always is – that you look at me and want me and I don't turn away.

If I want to say no, I will, but for the right reasons. If I want to say yes, I will, but for the right reasons. Leave the consequences. Leave the finale. Leave the grand statements. The simplicity of feeling should not be taxed. I can't work out what this will cost or what either of us owe. The admission charge is never on the door, but you are open and I want to enter.

Let me in.

You do.

In this space which is inside you and inside me I ask for no rights or territories. There are no frontiers or controls. The usual channels do not exist. This is the orderly anarchic space that no one can dictate, though everyone tries. This is a country without a ruler. I am free to come and go as I please. This is Utopia. It could never happen beyond bed. This is the model of government for the world. No one will vote for it, but everyone comes back here. This is the one place where everybody comes.

Most of us try to turn this into power. We're too scared to do anything else.

But it isn't power – it's sex.

Sex. How did it start?

In the strange dark history of our evolution, there was a shift, inevitability, away from self-reproducing organisms – like bacteria – towards organisms which must fuse with one another to survive.

You see, bacteria know the secret of eternal life. They do not die unless something kills them. They don't change, they don't age, all they do is multiply.

Fusion allows complexity and diversity, but with it, we don't know why, hand in hand, came death in the first of her many disguises. Death disguised as life.

It was our only chance. We took it.

So those morbid medievals and those burning Romantic poets weren't wrong. Sex and death belong together, joined in our imaginations as they are in our DNA.

Sex and death are our original parents. For some of us, the only family we'll ever have.

Sex. How did it start?

That hotel room in Paris. Dinner at Paul's. The walk over the bridge. Champagne in the afternoon. The rain. Your face.

And before that? Before I saw you?

I'm looking for something, it's true. Looking for you, looking for me, believing that the treasure is really there. I knew from the moment I saw you (as the saying goes) how it was going to begin.

I don't know how this will end.

'It's never enough for you, is it?' you said.

That was odd, because it was enough, just then. I pulled you down towards me, feeling your hair on my throat.

I said, 'If it's never enough, it's my fault not yours.'

She looked at me like I'm crazy. Most of my lovers do, and that's partly why they love me, and partly why they leave. I'm not being completely honest here because I do the leaving myself sometimes.

She said –

'We both want life. That's why I'm here.'

'You want risk.'

'What's wrong with that?'

'And you want safety.'

'What's wrong with that?'

'Don't you read the financial papers?'

'Never. I'm married to a banker.'

'You can't have safety and risk in the same investment.'

'You're not safe.'

'No, but your marriage is.'

'Listen, if I left my husband for you . . .'

'You think I'd leave you within the year.'

'Well, yes I do, if you really want to know.'

'Why do you say that?'

'You're not a sticker.'

'I'm not a quitter.'

'You want me because you can't have me.'

'Is that what you think?'

Heavy sighs. Bedclothes in a mess. Drink of water. Stare at ceiling.

'I had to have you that night in Paris.'

'Well done.'

'I never thought I'd see you again.'

'Did you want to see me again?'

'No.'

'But you went to Capri when you knew I would be there.'

'I wondered what would happen.'

'This is all a game, isn't it?'

'I wondered if you really could love me.'

'I don't understand.'

'I thought that if you could things might be different, things might change.'

'And have they changed?'

'Yes.'

'In what way?'

'I started to love you. I didn't expect that. My fault not yours.'

'And now?'

She ran her hands over me and there was something like surprise in her voice. She was telling the truth and that was hard. She looked away and said to me, 'It seems as though I've been caught in my own net.'

I turned and held her as close as I could.

'I never want to be your trap or snare.'

Then, because she was crying, I told her the Story of the Red Fox.

A hunter loved a Princess. Simple as that.

Every morning he brought her the treasures of the forest. He brought her deer and boar. He brought her wolf skin and buffalo hide. He fought a lion with his bare hands and caught the old black bear that everyone feared. He took nothing for himself. There was nothing he wanted except that she should love him, which she didn't.

One day, riding with her ladies, the Princess saw in front of them a red fox. Never was a fox so red. She watched it as it ran, stretching out its legs so that it seemed to be lying flat on the surface of the air. All day the fox stayed with the party and the Princess was troubled.

That night the Princess looked in the mirror and it seemed to her that the red of the fox would be perfect against the white of her skin. She stroked her neck and throat, imagining the feel of fox fur. Winter was coming.

When the hunter came to her the next morning, she said, 'If you love me, bring me the coat of the red fox.'

The hunter said, 'Ask me anything, but not that.'

'Then you do not love me,' said the Princess.

'I will hunt through the stars and shoot down the Lion and the Bull, but do not ask me for the red fox.'

The Princess was angry and turned away.

After many days and nights, when the snow had begun to fall, light as a promise, the hunter came to the Princess and promised to bring her the red fox. He had one condition.

'Say it.'
'The fox must be brought to you alive.'
'I accept the condition.'

The hunter left the palace and was not seen for three weeks. The weather became colder and the snow was as heavy as sorrow. When the Princess looked out she saw only white.

Or did she?

On the last morning of the third week the Princess looked out from her tower as usual and saw a streak of fire burning the snow. A quick red line made a way through the snow, melting it on either side, as if spring had come. Without pause or stop, moving from side to side and leaving no print, the red fox ran through the wastes of the snow until he came to the palace.

The Princess herself had begun to run too, down from her high tower, down the winding stairs, and out into the white courtyard, where the fox, panting in red steam, lay down at her feet.

The Princess put out her hand and the fox licked it as she bent down, and his eyes pleaded with her. She touched him and her white hand was buried in the thick warm fur, soft as blood.

Then she stood up and signalled to one of her men. Her face was clear and cold. She had the servant draw his knife, take the fox by the scruff, and then there was a second, only a second, when she hesitated, and looked for the last time at the brave pleading eyes and the strong head that offered no resistance.

The servant cut the throat out of the fox, and as the blood ran in a warm fountain across the icy cobbles of the courtyard, the servant staggered and fell under the weight of what he was holding. The fox had gone and the hunter lay dead in the yard.

You lay in my arms.

'I don't want to ask you for more than you can give,' you said.

'I'm the one who's asking.'

'We're both asking.'

'So what's the answer?'

'Not this.'

'It feels like an answer, when we're here, together.'

'There's a world outside.'

'Are you sure?'

'Don't start that stuff.'

'World or no world, I want you with me.'

'It's too intense. We'd wear each other out in six months.'

'Fire doesn't burn itself.'

'It burns out.'

'Listen, I don't want you to leave your marriage for me.'

'Getting tired already?'

'I want you to leave it for yourself.'

She got up. She hates this conversation and so do I. Why do we keep coming back to it like a crime we've committed?

I went after her, touched her shoulder, gently, sorry.

'I'll make us some lunch.'

I went into the kitchen. I love food. The clarity of it, the direct pleasure. I love it simple, absolutely fresh and freshly cooked. At my worst, like now, when nothing makes sense to myself, I'll cook something as a way of forcing order back into chaos. As a way of re-establishing myself, at least in this one thing. It steadies my hands.

SALSA DI POMODORI

Take a dozen plum tomatoes and slice them lengthways as though they were your enemy. Fasten them into a lidded pot and heat for ten minutes.

Chop an onion without tears.
Dice a carrot without regret.
Shard a celery stick as though its flutes and grooves were the indentations of your past.

Add to the tomatoes and cook unlidded for as long as it takes them to yield.

Throw in salt, pepper and a twist of sugar.

Pound the lot through a sieve or a mouli or a blender. Remember – they are the vegetables, you are the cook. Return to a soft flame and lubricate with olive oil. Add a spoonful at a time, stirring like an old witch, until you achieve the right balance of slippery firmness.

Serve on top of fresh spaghetti. Cover with rough new parmesan and cut basil. Raw emotion can be added now.

Serve. Eat. Reflect.

I put the steaming plate in front of her. She took a mouthful, then another.

'This is fantastic.'

'Food tastes better in Italian.'

Thickly, through a mouthful of spaghetti, she said, 'My husband is in Oxford.'

'Oh.'

'I have to go there today.'

'What about me?'

'I've told him about you. Well, not everything about you.'

'What exactly?'

'How we met in Paris.'

'I thought he didn't know you were in Paris?'

'I always tell him where I am, but not always who I'm with.'

'Does he put up with that?'

'We have an understanding.'

'I wish I did.'

'Look, a marriage has to survive in its own way.'

'What about the people inside the marriage?'

'It works for us.'

'OK. What about the people outside the marriage?'

'Nobody need get involved unless they want to.'

'Sounds simple on paper.'

'You're the writer.'

'Yes, and if I was writing this, I'd say . . .'

'Well, what *would* you say?'

I was silent. I have no superior wisdom and I want to avoid the self-righteousness that hides ignorance and fear. I've made so many mistakes myself that I'm not in a position to say, 'This is how it should be done.' Anyway, life is not a formula and love is not a recipe. The same ingredients cook up differently every time.

Take two people. Slice lengthways. Boil with the lid on. Add a marriage, a past, another woman. Sugar to taste. Pass through a chance meeting. Lubricate sparingly. Serve on a bed of – or is it in a bed of – ? Use fresh and top with raw emotion.

'I'd say that love slices lengthways.'

She was silent. We were both exposed. The truth is that you can divide your heart in all sorts of interesting ways – a little here, a little there, most banked at home, some of it coined out for a flutter. But love cleaves through the mind's mathematics. Love's lengthways splits the heart in two – the heart where you are, the heart where you want to be. How will you heal your heart when love has split it in two?

She said, 'I don't know. I don't know how this will end.'

We walked through the city with its Sunday feel of a sudden spaceship that has taken everyone to Mars.

There were no brokers, no bankers, no shops open. There was no one at the bus stop, no one flagging down a taxi. Occasionally a car would pass us, slow, curious, and there were two policewomen exercising their horses.

I have an odd sense of 'Where am I?' when I hear hooves on the road in a city. The buildings amplify the sound, and two horses at a trot sound like the cavalry. If I don't look round, it feels like the past coming up behind me, and I hear the rattle of the milk wagons, and the heavy wooden beer barrels coming off the drays, and the horse-drawn box that says SUNLIGHT SOAP.

Behind me, now, there'll be a man in a flat cap selling rolled-gold watches off a tray, and a boy shouting the latest headlines off a cart stacked with newspapers.

In front of me are the Bank of England, London Wall and a big red bus. I half turn, and if I don't see what I can hear behind me, I see the buildings – Edwardian, Victorian, Georgian. Old London is just above the shopfronts. The steel, plate glass and bright signs belong to me, but look up, just one storey, and the past is as solid as it ever was.

I wonder, maybe, if time stacks vertically, and there is no past, present, future, only simultaneous layers of reality. We experience our own reality at ground level. At a different level, time would be elsewhere. We would be elsewhere in time.

'If I could have my time again, I'd be with you.'

(Where have I heard that before?) 'You are with me.'

'I made choices before I met you.'

'The whole of life is more than a single decision.'

'Some decisions are more important than others.'

'This is one of them.'

'What do you mean?'

'I mean it's either/or.'

'You or him?'

'No. The same life or something different.'

'I like my life.'

'Fine. Keep it just as it is.'

'But that includes you.'

'No. No, it doesn't.'

I can't do it. I've been here before and it's not a room with a view. The only power I have is the negative power of withdrawal. If I don't withdraw I have no power at all. A relationship where one person has no power or negative power, isn't a relationship, it's the bond between master and slave.

'For God's sake, give me a break!'

'I'd have to break myself.'

And then I'm thinking, why am I like this? Why?

I think it's fair to say that my parents were not loved as children, that they did not love each other and that they did not love me. There was possession, fear, sentimentality, desire, but not love. This has left me with certain absences and certain intensities.

Absent is any real sense of family, of bonding, of belonging. Intensified is a longing for love as it really is — as freedom, abundance, generosity, passion. What Dante calls 'the love that moves the sun and the other stars'.

This love exists. Perhaps it is the only thing that exists. It is the buried treasure. The treasure is really there.

Fragments, hints, clues, letters, persuade me on. I've come near it sometimes, but like Lancelot outside the Chapel of the Grail, I haven't been able to go in. I may never be able to go in.

In your face, in your body, as you walk and lie down and eat and read, you have become the lineaments of love. When I touch you I touch something deeper than you. This touches something in me otherwise too sunk to recover.

I suffer. I intentionally put myself in the way of suffering as a test, as a measure, to see what will be drawn up – to stop myself from closing up. I don't want to close the wound.

Love wounds. There is no love that does not pierce the hands and feet. Love's exquisite happiness is also love's exquisite pain. I do not seek pain but there is pain. I do not seek suffering but there is suffering. It is better not to flinch, not to try and avoid those things in love's direction. It is not easy, this love, but only the impossible is worth the effort.

In the Grail legends Lancelot, the best knight in the world, never does see the Grail because he cannot give up his love for Guinevere. As a moral essay this suggests that human passion is no substitute for divine love and that it prevents us from experiencing love fully. This has been the basis of Christian thought since St Paul.

There is another reading. Lancelot fails, not because he can't give up Guinevere, but because he can't distinguish between love's symbol and what it represents. All human love is a dramatic enactment of the wild, reckless, unquenchable, undrainable love that powers the universe. If death is everywhere and inescapable, then so is love, if we but knew it. We can begin to know it through each other. The tamer my love, the farther away it is from love. In fierceness, in heat, in longing, in risk, I find something of love's nature. In my desire for you, I burn at the right temperature to walk through love's fire.

So when you ask me why I cannot love you more calmly, I answer that to love you calmly is not to love you at all.

SHOW BALLOONS

Once a year at the Muck House we opened our yard doors and went out, all three of us, into the Wilderness.

The Wilderness was a big place. It was everywhere and everything, except for the Muck House.

The expedition was carefully planned. Best clothes were worn, including hats, and we were allowed out between the hours of nine and six precisely. My father went into the Wilderness every day, but he was a man, and it was trade.

The day came. Hand in hand with my mother and father, I watched the great gates swing open. My father had oiled them the night before and taken down the barbed wire. Rigged to a car battery, the gates could open and shut themselves. Their silent sinister invitation pointed outwards towards . . .

'The Promised Land,' said my mother.

'I thought it was the Wilderness.'

'The only way to the Promised Land is through the Wilderness.'

'Then why don't we go there more often?'

'Temptations.'

Out we went.

We went past Woolworth's – 'A den of vice.' Past Marks & Spencer – 'Iniquity.' Past the Funeral Parlour and the doner kebab shop – 'They share an oven.' Past the biscuit stall and its moon-faced owners – 'Incest.' Past the dog-clipping salon – 'Bestiality.' Past the bank – 'Usury.' Past the Citizens' Advice Bureau – 'Communists.' Past the day nursery – 'Unmarried mothers.' Past the hairdresser's – 'Vanity.' Past the jeweller's where my mother had once tried to pawn her gold tooth, and on at last to a caff called the Palatine for beans on toast.

I was still worrying about the Promised Land.

'So the only way to the Promised Land is through the Wilderness, and when you get to the Promised Land, what do you find?'

'The buried treasure.'

'And what do you do with it when you've found it?'

'I don't know.'

'Why don't you know?'

'Because I've never found it.'

'Have you seen the Promised Land?'

'No.'

'Then how do you know there is one?'

'It's shown on the map.'

'What map?'
She thumped her heart.

She thumped her heart and looked away. She was such a mixture of cynicism and credulity. She believed what her heart told her, but she could never follow it. Her heart was like a bird that flew away and returned with stories in its beak. She heard, but she could not follow. Even the near places seemed too far. She had a bad leg. The Promised Land was farthest of all, but she knew it was there.

I watched the people going up and down the street, beyond the smoky glass of the Palatine caff. I wondered if I would have to spend forty years in the Wilderness before I found the Promised Land. And, after forty years, would I remember why I had set out?

We sat round the fire that night, Mother and Father and me. We sat like conspirators, firelight on our faces, fire in our hearts. We sat like angels on the edge of time, glowing and intense. We were on the wheel's rim of our desire. The circle we made was a charm against emptiness and a line drawn round hope. We dangled our feet into the black space of what might happen next.

We were talking about the treasure.

'When I was young,' my mother said, 'there was a hollow tree that had been struck by lightning, and anyone who crawled inside the trunk and dared to stand there for three minutes took away some of the lightning power. You could tell who they were because they had a glow about them. Wherever they walked afterwards, they'd find a penny that became a pound, or a key that opened a door.'

'Did you never stand in there yourself?' said my father.

'I did, and the money I found was this . . .' She reached her hand into the bucket of foreign coins. 'And the key I found was that.' She pointed to an old rusty key that hung like a reproach over the mantelpiece.

'That key fits nothing,' said my father.

'It's waiting for the door,' said my mother.

I looked at it closely. I had never looked at it before. Like all familiar objects it had become invisible. And what was there to look at? A rusty hoop, a rusty bar and a rusty block. It was just another six inches of rust in a house rusted with rust.

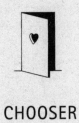

CHOOSER

'So now you know.'

    'Know what?'

    'Why I can't settle for less.'

    'Less is more.'

    'No, it's just less.'

    'Do you remember – in Paris . . .' (She hesitated.)

    'I remember everything about Paris.'

    'How you brushed the rain from the marble table . . .'

    'With my sleeve . . .'

    'And then you brushed the rain from my forehead . . .'

    'With my fingers . . .'

    'I wanted it to be your lips.'

    'So did I.'

    'You were hard to get.'

    'Not hard enough. I should have said no.'

    'Do you wish you had said no?'

    'No.'

We were silent. The kind of silent when there's nothing left to say.

'Kiss me.'

Yes. Always. Even when I never see you again. After speech, kisses. The silent movie of my feelings for you. Our lips say one thing and do another. We argue in English and make love in French. I kissed you and we were in that attic room again. Our private world. Our promised land.

This is what happens in the Bible story:

After forty years of wandering in the Wilderness, the chosen people come to the Promised Land. The grapes are so heavy that it takes two men to carry a single bunch. The cattle are the size of elephants. The land flowing with milk and honey is there, right there, in front of their eyes and just over the ridge. The Israelites can't believe their luck. This is it.

And then . . .

'If the grapes are as big as that, the wine will be too strong to drink.'

'Those cattle! Think how much they will need to eat!'

'I couldn't get my hand round the udders.'

'And the honey! Honey everywhere!'

'The bees must be gigantic.'

'Swarms of gigantic bees! Oy, oy, oy . . .'

'Mountain lions! Mountain lions love honey.'

'Locusts love honey.'

'People already live here.'

'They must be huge.'

'All that milk and honey. What a diet.'

'We'll be killed.'

'You know, the Wilderness isn't such a bad place.'

'It's windy, it's cold, it's barren, it's dusty . . .'

'There's a lot of sand.'

'But it isn't such a bad place.'

'Maybe we could find another Promised Land?'

'With less honey and smaller cows.'

'The boy's right. At least the Wilderness is ours.'

I said, 'You're going to walk away from this, aren't you?'

'I have to,' she said.

We took a taxi to Paddington Station. She had just missed a train to Oxford, so we sat in the Costa Coffee place and ordered cappuccino and *tortina*, and tried to talk above the house music and the station announcements. There wasn't much to say.

'We should have let it end in Paris.'

'Then it would have been nothing but a memory.'

'A happy memory,' she said.

'In Capri, it turned into a possibility.'

'I know.'

'A door opened. A door in a blank wall.'

'Love is a door in a blank wall.'

'Do you love me?'

'Yes.'

There was something I had to know.

'In Capri —'

'Yes . . .'

'When I came to find you —'

'Yes.'

'I was sure you wanted to risk it.'

'I did.'

'So what went wrong?'

'I did.'

'I don't understand.'

'I couldn't do it. I can't untangle my whole life.'

'And yet you came to London.'

'I had to see you again.'

'What's the problem? Is it money?'

'No.'

'Then what is it?'

'I can't be an exile from my own past.'

'I don't want your past.'

'That's just it. I can't start again at year zero.'

Railway station. Point of arrival. Point of departure. A transit zone. How light she looked, with just a suitcase she could carry in one hand. Inside that suitcase was a marriage, America, a life of which I knew nothing. Inside that suitcase were doors I had never opened into rooms I wouldn't recognise. The suitcase was stuffed with letters and an address book and a store card for a shopping mall, and dinner parties I had never been to, and wouldn't go to now. In that suitcase were invitations from friends and pre-sets on a car radio tuned to stations I had never heard. In that suitcase were bad dreams and secret hopes. The dirty linen was in a special nylon compartment. Her childhood was in there – the awkward child with rough plaits who grew into a beautiful heavy-haired woman, who never quite believed the compliments of the mirror. Her husband was in there, or maybe he was strapped to the side, where you usually keep the lifeboats.

I looked at the suitcase, suddenly heavy, too heavy to carry, and I realised that she could never drag it with her. She was right – it would have to be let go, or taken home and unpacked again.

'Let's just walk away,' I said.

'Weren't you listening?'

'Yes. I mean both of us. Together. You from your life. Me from mine.'

'What are you saying?'

'I'll leave everything behind too.'

'You're crazy.'

'I can work anywhere. I can sell my house.'

'Where would we go?'

'Italy? Ireland? Where do you want to go? Paris?'

'You can't do that.'

'I can. I will. If you will.'

What should stop me? What does a person need in this life except a roof, food, work and love? Here was the person I loved. I am able to work. Where the roof is and where the food is doesn't matter.

'If you'll give up your past, I'll give up mine,' I said.

(She looked at her suitcase.)

'I'll bring clothes, books and the cat. That's all.'

(Her suitcase was getting bigger.)

'We can start again with furniture. We can make new friends.'

(The suitcase was filling up the coffee house.)

'We'll rent an apartment overlooking the river.'

(The suitcase was pressing against the walls.)

'With a bed and a chair and the morning sun.'

(The suitcase was pressing against my chest.)

'When we open the windows, we'll be like birds.'

(The suitcase was in my ribcage.)

'Our happiness will be like the flight of birds.'

There was an announcement. The 4.15 to Oxford was standing

at Platform 9. You stood up. You picked up your case.

We walked to the dirty hissing train and found you a seat opposite a Walkman wearer and a woman reading *Hello!* magazine. This is the emotional and cultural life of the nation. No wonder grand gestures fall flat. How can you say yes when everything around you is saying no?

If you had said yes, I would have been scared to death, and it might have been a mistake, but I would have done my part. How can you go back? How can I? I'll probably sell my house now anyway. My life doesn't make sense. Starting again, as clean as I can, is the only way I'm going to make sense of it. The train, the station, the noise, are meaningless. Your leaving is absurd. I can't stand it. I sit down and take your hand.

'Come with me. Come with me now.'

Here are two endings. You choose.

Two minutes to go. I'm holding your hand. The woman reading *Hello!* magazine is clearly disgusted at the sight of real feeling and gets up to sit elsewhere. The Walkman boy props his feet on her seat.

The train is leaving, leaving now, and you won't meet my eyes. I can't come with you. You're not coming with me. The whistle blows. I have to jump up, forcing apart the closing doors. Then I'm outside again, walking down the platform, walking faster and faster, miming at you to pull the emergency cord. Just pull it. The train will stop. You can get off, leave your bag, and come with me. I'm running now. There's still time, still time. Then there's a moment when time is so still it stops and the train moves ahead for ever.

Two minutes to go. I'm holding your hand. The woman reading *Hello!* magazine smiles at me. She's sorry for me.

You're looking at me and there's still a chance. Dear love, risk everything, there is no other way.

The whistle blows. I stand up, still holding your hand, and suddenly you're on your feet, and we're both out of the closing door as it shuts on your past, shuts on your suitcase, and the woman is miming desperately that you've left your bag.

The train is gathering speed now, taking time with it, and we've found a second where there is no time. The second that beats between your life and mine.

Then the clock is ticking again, but we're together. The train moves ahead without us.

strange

Night.

I'm sitting at my screen reading this story. In turn, the story reads me.

Did I write this story, or was it you, writing through me, the way the sun sparks the fire through a piece of glass?

I see through a glass darkly. I cannot tell whether the moving shapes are on the other side, or whether they are behind me, beside me, reflected in the room.

I cannot give my position accurately. The co-ordinates shift. I cannot say, 'Where,' I can only say, 'Here,' and hope to describe it to you, atom and dream.

Why did I begin as I did, with Ali and the tulip?

I wanted to make a slot in time. To use time fully I use it vertically. One life is not enough. I use the past as a stalking horse to come nearer to my quarry.

My quarry is you and me, caught in time, running as fast as we can.

To avoid discovery I stay on the run. To discover things for myself, I stay on the run.

Here's my life, steel-hitched at one end into my mother's belly, then thrown out across nothing, like an Indian rope trick. Continually I cut and retie the rope. I haul myself up, slither down. What keeps the tension is the tension itself – the pull between what I am and what I can become. The tug of war between the world I inherit and the world I invent.

I keep pulling at the rope. I keep pulling at life as hard as I can. If the rope starts to fray in places, it doesn't matter. I am so tightly folded, like a fern or an ammonite, that as I unravel, the actual and the imagined unloose together, just as they are spliced together – life's fibres knotted into time.

Gently the rope swings back and forth through the mirror, through the screen.

What is my life? Just a rope slung across space.

QUIT

Poor Ali. What happened to him? He never did deliver his bulbs to the Botanic Garden at Leiden. He bought a piece of land by the river and planted a pleasure garden for the ladies of Holland.

Tulip mania is well documented. Any economics textbook or gardening history will tell you that. And tell you too of the tulip's later success in England, 'where many partake of the delight of this noble flower'.

Ali's story is not well documented, and the uses found by the ladies of Holland for this amorous flower have been kept a close secret.

A Dutch lady, Mrs van der Pluijm, taught the Earl of Hackney's daughter how best to arrange her bulbs and stem and the practice soon spread. Few men were aware of their wives' and daughters' true passion for this Exotic from the East, and as men are apt to try and please women, and love to gamble, it was easy enough to whip a craving into a craze.

When Ali unstrapped her bulbs and planted them in the good earth, she was obeying the command of the scriptures to go forth and multiply. Multiply she did – bulbs, balls, fortune and friends – for every lady of fashion longed to walk in the gently nodding garden and lie under a tree, where she could experience for herself those exquisite attributes of variation that humans and tulips share.

There is some pictorial evidence to suggest that one man, at least, knew what was going on.

Rembrandt's 1633 painting of his wife Saskia, as Flora, goddess of abundance and fertility, pictures Saskia/Flora holding a bridal bouquet suggestively near her pleasure-parts. In the centre of the bouquet, its head raised, is an opening tulip.

Rembrandt. During his lifetime he painted himself at least fifty times, scribbled numerous drawings and left twenty etchings. No artist had done this before. No artist had so conspicuously made himself both the subject and object of his work.

The picture changes all the time. He dresses up, wears armour, throws on a hat or a cloak. The face ages, wrinkles, smoothes out again. These are not photographs, these are theatre.

Why did Rembrandt use himself as his own prop?

Well, because he was there, but, just as importantly, because he wasn't there. He was shifting his own boundaries. He was inching into other selves. These self-portraits are a record, not of one life, but of many lives – lives piled in on one another, and sometimes surfacing through the painter and into paint.

The fixed point is the artist himself, about whom we know

enough to write a biography. But the fixed point is only the base camp — the journeys out from there are what interests. Rembrandt's pictures are the journeys out and the psychic distance travelled can be measured as light.

Light made a palette of dark and shade out of Ali's face as he slept. Was he back in Turkey, tending his mother's eggplants and tomatoes? He might have been there, nervously dressed as a boy, telling his stories as tall as he was short.

The stories he told made him too old to be alive. Some made him not yet born. He slipped between the gaps in history as easily as a coin rolls between the floorboards. Ask him about anything and it's himself he'll produce, dusty but triumphant — the piece of good luck, the hidden observer, in the right place at the right time.

Ali tells stories for a living. Someone has to do it. Stories are his bread and butter and he carries a slice in his pocket, to eat himself or to offer to others. He shares all he has, then goes home to make more.

It has not been proved, but it might be so, that Ali is not telling stories, but that the stories are telling him. As he knots himself into a history that never happened and a future that cannot have happened, he is like a cross-legged Turk who knots a fine carpet and finds himself in the pattern.

As Ali knots himself into time, he has wondered if St

Augustine might be right. A Catholic, who taught Ali to read, taught him that St Augustine had said that the universe was not created *in* time but *with* time.

This is true of the stories. They have no date. We can say when they were written or told, but they have no date. Stories are simultaneous with time.

Ali the storyteller is no longer sure when things happen. The happening and the telling seem to be tumbling over and over each other, like the acrobats who used to visit his village, turning their red and blue legs like the spokes of a wheel, round and round, faster and faster.

Ali is not a fool. He knows what day it is and that one day he will die. He knows how much money he has and how to avoid the people who would take it off him. He knows where he lives and the name of his little dog.

What he doesn't know, really doesn't know, is where he begins and the stories end. How can he know? The people who think they know define reality according to what is obvious and advise Ali to do the same. He would, gladly, but while what is obvious to them is also obvious to him, what is obvious to him is not obvious to them.

Ali tells stories. He puts himself in the stories. Once there, he cannot easily get out again, and the stories he has told cook up with the dinner he is eating and wrap round the sheets on the bed. What he is, what he invents, becomes part of the same story, one continuous story, where even birth and death are only markers, pauses, changes of tempo. Birth and death become new languages, that is all.

The obvious people shake their heads, and say that when Ali is in his grave, that will be an end to his stories and an end to him.

Will it? Or will it be a shift to other mouths and other tales, while Ali, with his tale in his mouth, rolls on?

REALLY QUIT?

The Map. The Treasure.

In 1460 Giovanni da Castro, godson of Pope Pius II, returned to Italy from the Levant.

In his memoirs, Pius himself described what happened.

While Giovanni was walking through the forested mountains, he came on a strange kind of herb. He was surprised and noted that similar herbs grew on mountains of Asia which enrich the Turkish treasury with alum. He also observed white stones which appeared to have mineral in them. He bit one of them and found them salt. He smelted them, experimented and produced alum.

He then went to the Pope and said, 'Today I bring you victory over the Turk. Every year they wring from the Christians more than 300,000 ducats for the alum with which we dye wool various colours. For alum is not found in Italy except a very small quantity in the island of Ischia near Puteoli, and this supply was depleted by the Romans in ancient times and is almost exhausted.

'But I have found seven mountains so rich in this material that they could supply seven worlds . . .'

Giovanni takes up the story himself.

All day I had been searching for a pearl earring lost in my chamber by my mistress. At evening, restless and despondent, I could think of nothing at all. I walked out to brood on this life of ours, which seems from birth to death to be a steady loss, disguised by sudden gains and happiness, which persuade us of good fortune, when all the while the glass is emptying.

'Eat stones for bread,' I said to myself, and picking up a rock began to gnaw it. It was salty. It was then that I began my explorations of the mountain.

Imagine my surprise when I found not one mountain but seven, each supplying in abundance what we had most needed and most lacked. I have walked in these mountains since I was a child. Since I was a child I have walked back and forth over the riches and prospect for which I had dreamed.

Everything I had sought had been under my feet from the beginning.

The world is a mirror of the mind's abundance

RESTART

The Map. The Treasure.

There's no Netscape Navigator to help me find my way around life. I have to do it myself and my helpers are unexpected and odd. Of course, I can take a planned route, like those things you buy on the highway to tell you which way to go. There are plenty of organised tours and arranged excursions. I need miss no Ancient Monument or World Heritage Site. I can even go off-track, provided I follow the way-markers. If I want to go on safari, I can do it from the safety of a jeep, but I must not, must not, get out and stare at the lions.

Why not?

They will eat me.

A lion did eat a tourist recently. The lion was then trapped and shot, and when the hunters cut him open they found a whole leg, foot and training shoe in his stomach. Also a booklet warning the tourist about the danger of lions.

Lions are dangerous. True.

Lions live in the Wilderness. True.

How else am I going to find the Promised Land, if not by way of the lions?

There's no guarantee that I will find what I'm looking for. Should that deter me? We all want guarantees these days – for rising damp, bank deposits, washing machines, computer compliance, pedigree status, stain remover, marriage and torch batteries. Is this because life comes with no guarantees at all?

There are no guarantees. I just have to risk it.

There was a day, years and years ago, when I tried to escape from the Muck House. I took a ladder and leaned it against the high wall that kept us in and the world out. I was three rungs away from the top of the ladder when I felt it shake down below. I didn't need to look down to know that my mother was trying to shake me off like an apple from a tree.

'Get down here!'

I got down, and as I hit the ground my mother hit me twice across the face.

'What do you think you were playing at?'

'I wanted to see the Wilderness.'

'There's nothing there. You know that.'

'If there's nothing there, it can't harm me.'

'Nothing is the most dangerous thing of all.'

'Why?'

'If there's nothing there, you can invent something. You won't be able to bear the emptiness. It will still be empty, but you'll tell yourself it's not.'

'What I tell myself is true.'

'What you tell yourself is a story.'

'This is a story – you, me, the Muck House, the treasure.'

'This is real life.'

'How do you know?'

'No one would ever pay to watch it.'

She turned to go in to the battered house. Then she turned to me again.

'And I would pay anything not to live it.'

'Don't live it. Change it.'

'You don't understand, do you?'

'Understand what?'

'This is real life.'

And I thought of us, years and years later, you and I, in Paris, and how you seemed to be saying we had every choice, every chance. You acted as though you were free, but you were a ransom note. I paid to watch. I watched your fingers, your red mouth. I watched you undress. I didn't see you go.

Later I was still paying and I never counted the cost. You were worth it. Again and again you were worth it. My heart has unlimited funds. Draw on them. Draw them down. Draw me down on top of you. How much? Everything? All right.

The glittering river and the soft evening were a promise. The world had just begun. It was only a day old. It was the day we met. The promise is that the world is always beginning again. No accumulations of the past can stop it. Another day. Another chance.

Does nobody believe this? You didn't. Nothing I offered could free you because you couldn't free yourself. You were wayward, but you still wanted to follow the path.

I thought of us, that afternoon in Paris, after we had escaped from the rain. The sun came out and the pavements shone. It was as though the streets had been silvered into a mirror, and we could see the buildings and the statues and our own faces multiplied by the glass pyramid of the Louvre and the smooth flat mirror of the rain.

It was after the flood. The past had been drowned, but we had been saved. In the multiple possibilities of the mirror we could have taken any direction we wanted.

Drops of rain fell from the hem of our coats and from the falling weight of your hair. Each one was a complete world, a crystal ball of chance that held our future. Let them fall. There were so many, so many chances, so many futures. When I brushed away the rain from your forehead, aeons broke back into the waters where they were made. We were universes dripping with worlds. All we had to do was choose.

'Noah must have felt like this.'

'Soaked?'

'Free.'

Imagine it.

The floodwaters subside and the ark comes to rest on top of Mount Ararat. The dove returns with an olive branch in her mouth.

Imagine it. Years and years later, the ground is long since dry and fertile, and the boat is still up there, beached on its mountain-top like a memory point.

I look back on it, amazed. I can hardly believe it is there – absurd, impossible testimony to something that never happens.

But it did happen. It happened to us.

Many waters cannot quench love, neither can floods drown it.

Through the streets, you and I, hand in hand, like a pair of twins spun out of the constellations.

The earth was all before us. The day was innocent of past and future. There were no decisions, no reminders, just the day and us in it.

Two Buddhists in saffron robes were chanting and dancing in front of a portable shrine.

'Be here now,' you said.

'What?'

'The Buddhist Way.'

I laughed. I knew you were right. You spent the day convincing me that you were right, and when I slept with you it was in that nowness, that rightness.

Through the streets, you and I, and our footprints seemed to burn in the water. The steam rose up round us as we walked, as though our feet had been shod.

Shod or branded? You marked me that day and nothing can cool the wound.

SAVE

Night.

I'm at home in Spitalfields. I live above the shop. The sign on the shop just says VERDE and no one can see inside. The big windows in their old wooden frames have blinds pulled down over the lower panes. The clock ticks, but only in time. There are shadows on the ceiling – a bear's head, a knife.

In a minute I'll go downstairs into the shop and start pinning up a story somebody wants for tomorrow. I hope it fits.

Meanwhile the City boys, with their home-time faces, are loosening their ties, forgetting the closing price of Internet stocks and looking for a drink. The deli next door is still slicing Parma ham. I can hear the whirr of the blade as I go downstairs.

A quick glance outside and there's the Hawksmoor church, and the ABN bank, and the little man with his coffee van, packing up to go home. In the huge spaces of the abandoned market, off-duty traders are playing softball.

I shut the door just in time to avoid the Jack the Ripper

Tour. My house is on the route, and students and pensioners and earnest Americans in track shoes huddle together outside the shopfront, staring at the old notices on the shutters, gazing in fascination at the front door, half-believing that the Ripper will come out, dressed as a midwife or a nurse or an oyster seller, or whatever disguises he took from all the disguises inside.

Across the road, the Dracula Tour is warming up. Why, I don't know. Spitalfields is nowhere near Transylvania or Whitby, and even in Roman times, it never had a sea coast.

But this is an old house.

The first night I slept here, I slept in the basement. Somewhere in the uncertain hours of the night, I heard footsteps clattering down the stairs. I sat up and called out — 'Who is that?'

No answer. I lay back, certain that I was not alone, and then a hand gently took hold of mine, just above the wrist, on the pulse. After a moment, as if to see which one of us was alive, the hand let go of mine, and whatever it was stood by the bed, breathing.

This is an old house.

If you were to come here, forgetting about time, and ringing the bell as the afternoon ends, you would find the shop as it has always been — keeping its secrets, offering you something that money can't buy — freedom just for one night.

You would stand alone in the shop, looking at the suits of

armour, the field boots and the wimples and the wigs on spikes, like severed heads. Then I'd be there, smiling at you, waiting. Waiting for the moment to begin.

You say you want to be transformed.

Downstairs, I switched on the screen and watched the familiar blank space surface towards me to be filled. Blank spaces are my domain.

Here's the story . . .

The rain was thick as glass. For many days I had eaten, drunk, slept, walked, cased in glass. I felt like the relic of a saint. I felt like an Eastern curiosity. I stared out of the running walls of my prison, able to move, unable to escape.

In the forest every solid thing was changing into its watery equivalent. Whatever I grasped for purchase – root, branch, rock – slipped its hold. My fingers closed on nothing. The leaf-deep forest floor was a moving raft of brown water. The trees were water columns. In the liquid forest, I was the only solid thing and already my outline was beginning to blend with other outlines that were not me. I said my name again and again – 'ORLANDO! ORLANDO!'

I hoped my name would contain me, but the sound itself seemed to run off my tongue, and drop, letter by letter, into the pool at my feet. I tried again, but when I put my hand down into the pool of water, my name was gone.

'What am I doing here?'

The woman I love rode this way, carried off by horsemen. If I do not find her I will never find myself. If I do not find her, I will die in this forest, water within water.

What's that up ahead through the trees?

I came to a palace. There were no dogs, no sentries, and the way was open. I ran the back of my hand over my eyes, flicking off the rain, which was lighter now, and bearable. As I hesitated by the great iron gates, I heard her calling my name – 'ORLANDO! ORLANDO!' I hesitated no longer, and rushed inside the palace, sword drawn, ready for death, ready for life, sensing myself again, knowing my own name.

The palace was deserted. I leapt up the staircase, kicking open doors, shouting, wheeling, pausing, listening. Her captors must have abandoned her here. There was no danger. All I had to do was find her.

Room by room. Stable, courtyard, loggia, dungeon, tower, kitchen, scullery, armoury, library, larders, wine-presses, vaults, chapel, gun-room, tack-room, fishponds, barns, winter closets, summerhouse, servant's quarters, cell.

I was no longer sure where the rooms ended and I began. I seemed to be ransacking myself. Every door I opened was a confrontation with emptiness. Some of the rooms were furnished. Some were not. All were empty.

Or were they?

After a long time I noticed other figures, swords drawn, as intent as I was on searching the castle.

There was a man who lifted up tapestries – every tapestry every day – some by creeping forward and taking the corner with his finger and thumb, some with a rip or a yell or a stab. I passed him every third day, at noon, on the third staircase. He never glanced at me.

I soon realised that each of us had our own system, devised in fitful bouts of eating or resting. Each of us, solitary, intent, had made the palace into a personal labyrinth. We knew it better than the body of a lover. We knew it better than ourselves. It was ourselves. To each of us the palace had a secret meaning unrevealed to the rest.

And I will tell you a strange thing: whenever one of us turned to leave, wearied and desperate, for the doors were always open and no one was a prisoner here – that man would see, for a moment, a vision of what he sought – his lady, his falcon, his horse, the band of robbers who had fired his house. He would hear a voice, begging him, imploring him, taunting him, so that at the second when he would have abandoned his maze, he returned again, excited, convinced, to search the fishpond, the loggia, the scullery, the closet, the . . .

I tell you this; the palace was empty. That is, it was empty of what is sought, and filled only with seekers.

There was a day when a different kind of man came to the palace. Like us all, he had been lured there by a vision of his desire. He was chasing a peasant boy who had stolen his horse. When Astolfo came panting up to the palace, he knew at once that it was enchanted. Everywhere he looked, he saw one man, then another, ignoring all the rest, all running like fools down corridors without sense.

Astolfo lifted up the marble step at the main door and the entire palace vanished. Vanished completely.

You might think that would have made him a hero, but enchantment is not so easily dissolved. As we looked in amazement at the empty fields around us, we suddenly discovered in Astolfo the thing we had each sought in vain for so long. Some of us tried to make love to him, others of us tried to kill him. Poor man, he was half-dead of our attentions before he managed to pull out a whistle and blow a sharp blast.

That was the end of it. The note pierced through the last of our deceptions and we saw how it was. We didn't say much. We hardly glanced at each other as we took our own ways, some to the east, some to the west, some to the mountains, some to their own cities again.

I was the last to leave.

I put out my hand and felt the vanished walls. The palace was gone, or rather, it was no longer outside myself. The stairs, corridors, halls, rooms, the table candles, even the mustard pot I had thrown out of the refectory window, all had folded up again into the hiding places of the mind.

I was alone. Atom and dream.

The screen had dimmed. The room was deep in shadows, there were sounds outside, but I did not recognise them. The world had folded up and I thought we were back on the river again, watching the light-bands of the Friday-night cars. I could see the brown churn of the river and the grey heavy stone going down into it under the quay. It's always deeper than you think. Nobody gets to the bottom, and sometimes, when the tide is out, there's a flintlock, or a sword, or an earring, or a piece of Roman tessera, or a story.

Yes, always a story, sieved up out of the river.

A couple of years ago I went down to the Thames at the lowest tide of the century. 19 January 1998. The wide river had shrunk to a thin metal band. I walked down to where the water should have been, and it felt as though the invisible river had closed over me. I thought I was walking inside it.

Underneath my feet, at every step, there was a hard

crunching. Nervously I dipped my fingers into the silt and uncovered a handful of round balls, with the filmy look of a retina. They were bottle stoppers, the marbles used as bottle stoppers in the nineteenth century. I put them in my pocket, little capsules of the past, and walked on.

Perhaps this is how it is – life flowing smoothly over memory and history, the past returning or not, depending on the tide. History is a collection of found objects washed up through time. Goods, ideas, personalities surface towards us, then sink away. Some we hook out, others we ignore, and as the pattern changes, so does the meaning. We cannot rely on the facts. Time, which returns everything, changes everything.

A freak tide like this one uncovers more than we bargained for. Explanations drain away. Life is what it really is – a jumble, a chance, the upturned room of a madman. Out there I can see a fridge with its door off, and a coil of barbed wire, and a shopping trolley someone shoved off the bridge. I can see the heavy anchors patina'd with rust and decorated with barnacles. There are the rotten wooden pilings of old London – the driven stakes where the boats used to tie up. Now the pilings look like plugs of tobacco, brown and crumbling and moist.

Underneath there, for sure, will be the broken barrel of a pistol and a cache of oyster shells. There'll be a clay pipe and a billiard ball, and a bundle of abandoned clothes. The end of one identity, the beginning of another.

Explanations drain away. History is a madman's museum. I

think I know. I think I understand, but it's all subject to the tide.

Night. The screen is sleeping but I can't. I pick up my coat, go out of the door and walk down to the Thames.

The tide will be out.

In the middle of the river there's a light. I think I can get to it, past the hospital bed with its rubber castors missing, past the sea chest, still padlocked. Past the baby's cot and the armful of beer glasses. Here I go, negotiating the chip wrappers and the grinning broken glass. Here I go, wading into the water now, too far out.

The light is there, but it's not shining down, it's shining up. It's in the silt, in the red of the river, making a vertical shaft from the bottom to the surface.

This is a dirty river. Centuries have been pumped into it. This is the past pumped through time and taken out to sea. Mammoths used to drink from the shallow sandbanks. This is a Roman river, an Elizabethan river. This is the route to the Millennium Dome.

I dipped my hands in the water. Liquid time.

And I thought, 'Go home and write the story again. Keep writing it because one day she will read it.'

You can change the story. You are the story.

No date line, no meridian, no gas-burnt stars, no transit of the planets, not the orbit of the earth nor the sun's red galaxy, tell time here. Love is keeper of the clocks.

I took off my watch and dropped it into the water.

Time take it.

Your face, your hands, the movement of your body . . .

Your body is my Book of Hours.

Open it. Read it.

This is the true history of the world.